The LONG SEASON

Sam Brown

POCKET BOOKS

New York   London   Toronto   Sydney   Singapore

This book is a work of fiction. Names, characters, places, and incidents are either the product of the author's imagination or are used fictitiously. Any resemblance to actual events or locales or persons, living or dead, is entirely coincidental.

 POCKET BOOKS, a division of Simon & Schuster, Inc.
1230 Avenue of the Americas, New York, NY 10020

ISBN: 0-671-67186-3

First Pocket Books printing February 1991

12 11 10 9 8 7 6 5 4 3

POCKET and colophon are registered trademarks of Simon & Schuster, Inc.

For information regarding special discounts for bulk purchases, please contact Simon & Schuster Special Sales at 1-800-456-6798 or business@simonandschuster.com

Printed in the U.S.A.

Books by Sam Brown

The Big Lonely
The Crime of Coy Bell
The Long Season
The Trail of Honk Ballard's Bones

Published by POCKET BOOKS

FIGHTERS ON THE RANGE ...

JESSE COLDIRON: Once a carefree cowboy, he now had a mission. And he vowed that J. W. Cain would never take from him like he'd taken from others . . .

J. W. CAIN: A big-time cattle rustler careful to steal only from the small and powerless, he made his mistake when he took Jesse Coldiron's silence for cowardice . . .

TRACEY JAMES: Cruel tragedy had made the young widow distrustful of men. But when Jesse Coldiron stirred feelings she thought had died, she distrusted herself most of all . . .

HARLAN HARRELL: To protect and defend had been his reasons for living. Now, for Jesse Coldiron's old saddle partner, they seemed just reasons for dying—in a showdown with J. W. Cain . . .

"Fast-paced . . . grace, style and humor . . . Reminiscent of Jack Schaefer's working-class cowboy classic *Monte Walsh* . . . A dash of romance adds sparkle to *THE LONG SEASON*."
—*ALA Booklist*

"An authentic, exciting, satisfying novel of Texas life . . . Sam Brown's effort is welcome."
—*Library Journal*

The LONG SEASON

PROLOGUE

The meek shall inherit the earth.

Whatever the time and place when that prophecy was meant to be fulfilled, it was not in Oldham County, Texas, in 1884. Not in the open range country that the Canadian River sliced through; not in the sandhills and the sandy creeks; not in the scattered mesquite thickets or flats covered with tall tobosa grass and sinkholes; not among the deep, rocky-sided canyons rimmed with scrub cedar and cholla cactus; and not where the gray, red, and lavender cliffs of Tecovas and Trujillo formations locked away the petrified bones and teeth of creatures two hundred million years dead. In that world, the hunter reigned; tooth and claw ruled, and the meek were devoured.

Oldham County—like all of the West, from the Mississippi River to the Pacific Ocean—was locked in a hard season. A hard season not only of frost and snow—for these would pass, come again and pass again—but a longer, harder season of struggle against even less compassionate forces on both sides of the law. A struggle to see who would possess the land and its riches. A struggle between those who were in a position to make laws tailored to fit their special interests and those who obeyed only the laws of greed and gluttony.

Caught in between those two groups was a class of simple, honest, hard-working men and a few women who were used by both sides. One side wanted to rob and steal from them and to ride roughshod over them. The other side expected them to live under a legal system built on the same foundations as were the storehouses of the wealthy. Like hard-used work horses, these people were expected by both sides to lean into their collars without balking. Most did.

A few did not. They fought both sides. Sometimes they fought for the only thing they had left to fight for—principles. They bled and died. They won and lost. But they did not take the collar.

CHAPTER
1

A coyote, with long, tawny fur rushing toward full-prime, sat on his haunches, and as a king surveys his kingdom, so the animal surveyed his. His throne was a hilltop overlooking a long, wide draw, not unlike many other hilltops overlooking many other long and wide draws on that prairie. His refined, intelligent head slowly turned, stopping now and again to momentarily perk short ears. But nothing stirred, nor looked out of place enough to hold those sharp eyes longer than a few seconds. After a while the coyote heaved a sigh of boredom, curled up among the sagebrush that adorned his throne and went to sleep, temporarily disappearing from the landscape.

After he had vanished, the world for miles around seemed lifeless, dreary. No brilliant fall sun lent to the plains its magic of separating different hues and shades, of creating soft colors and bright, of casting shadows and giving outline. Instead, the gray of the sage-covered prairie rolled into the distance and blended with the gray of the leaden, low sky until the

3

far horizons were smudged into drab obscurity where neither earth nor sky could be distinguished for certain.

Thus passed the afternoon on a certain stretch of nameless prairie on the twentieth of November, 1884.

Perhaps, after three hours of undisturbed sleep, king coyote grew hungry and decided to rise, stretch, and then trot across two draws to take supper at the local dead cow. Or perhaps some inner sense told him to arise, stretch, and survey his kingdom once again, for there were sojourners passing through it. At any rate, he rose, stretched, took two quick steps, stopped short, perked those short ears northward, claimed his haunches once again, and kept his keen eyes on the hills to the north.

For half an hour he sat there, content to watch a dark figure come into sight atop one hill faraway, only to disappear and then reappear on the next closest hilltop. This continued unabated in silence and gradually dimming light until the dark figure separated into two, ever-growing closer and closer. Out of curiosity the coyote continued to watch. Sometimes he lay on his belly with only his head above the sage, sometimes he stood on all fours, sometimes down on his haunches again, but all the while he watched.

The two dark figures at last became two horses, both burdened—one with man, the other with clanging man-things. When man and horses stopped on the very next hilltop, the coyote tested the north breeze with his black-tipped nose, trotted halfway down his throne, and then stopped to inspect them again.

The man slipped off his leather gloves, pulled his makings from a coat pocket, and began rolling a cigarette, seeing the coyote on the next hillside but paying him no mind. He had other things to think about.

The man had had a long and unsuccessful day, and he was tired and disgusted. Had it been possible, the Jesse Coldiron out there in the middle of nowhere looking for a herd of lost heifers would have stepped apart from the Jesse Coldiron who had been foolish enough to let a fall blizzard catch his cattle on the open prairie and kick the living daylights out of him.

But that was not possible, so Jesse Coldiron had settled for the next best option—loud and particularly profane cussing of Jesse Coldiron. And he had been exercising that option at irregular intervals over the past four days and three nights.

How could a man who had cowboyed as long as he be so stupid, especially with his own cattle? The question popped into his mind time and again. He had a good canyon picked out to winter in, just inside Colorado. Plenty of grass and plenty of running water. All he had to do was to drive the heifers into it, set up camp in the cabin at its mouth, and sit out the long winter months while his heifers bellied down with their first calves.

He had felt so sure of a couple more weeks of open weather that he was still grazing the heifers on the plains when the first snowflakes came without warning, driven by a fierce northwest wind that gained momentum as it slid down the eastern slope of the Rockies. By then it was too late to do anything but hole-up until the storm howled itself out. That howling lasted two days—during which time it snowed in every way known. Then, just as suddenly as the snow and the wind struck, they stopped. Before the last flake had settled in, Jesse was jerking the latigo on the big brown gelding and leaving the Colorado foothills in a southeasterly direction, a little dun packhorse in tow.

He cut across the southwestern corner of No Man's Land and entered the Texas Panhandle. He had hopes, then, of overtaking the drifting herd that first day. He had not. And now the second day was drawing to a cold close and he had still seen neither hoof nor hide of that which had consumed so much of the last several years of his life.

To be sure, he had seen plenty of cattle—so many that picking out the tracks of his particular cattle would not have been possible even if the snow had not played out a few miles back. Plenty of cattle, but none of them his.

To confound matters even more, it was snowing lightly again, the north breeze was getting ominously colder, and other than knowing he was somewhere in the Texas Panhandle north of the Canadian River, he was not sure where he was.

Jesse Coldiron was still rolling a cigarette as he thought about these things and hoped to God—or to the devil or whoever was in charge of such things—that the increasing bite to the breeze and the light snow were only a temporary setback, and not the icy fingertips of another Arctic hand preparing to slap the plains senseless. As he raised the cigarette to his mouth to lick it, the brown gelding tossed his head, jerking the bridle reins and spilling the tobacco.

That was the last straw. Jesse Coldiron was now pushed past disgust and into aggravation. And he was suddenly aggravated at everything he could think of. He was aggravated at himself and the weather. He was aggravated at a bunch of springing Hereford-Longhorn crossbred heifers for not staying put. He was aggravated at all the big cow outfits in the world just for general principles. And most of all, he was aggravated at head-tossing brown geldings.

By process of elimination, it appeared the single brown gelding between his knees would receive the brunt of the retributions for all Jesse's aggravations. For after all, he *was* the handiest to get to, and his *was* the last aggravation bestowed upon the man, and the one most prominent in his temper. However, just at the moment when the brown's head was to be "tore off" something unusual in man-horse relations occurred—it didn't happen. Instead, the man turned in the saddle, faced the cold breeze and the light snow and bellowed at the top of his lungs: "Ha! Ha! Goddamn snow! Goddamn piggy heifers! Goddamn big rich outfits! Ha! Ha! Double goddamn head-slinging horses!"

This sudden outburst into a quiet, late afternoon had three immediate results: The man who rendered it felt a bit of relief; the brown gelding held his head dead-still except for a nervous flicking of the ears back and forth; king coyote dropped his tail and lit a shuck for a new kingdom.

Jesse Coldiron was a cowboy. From the top of his dirty gray hat to the bottom of his high-topped, high-heeled boots. He was a few months shy of forty and had cowboyed for a living for a quarter of a century. From the brushy breaks of South Texas to the wind-swept reaches of Montana, he had done and seen about all a twister could do and see and survive. He had made some of the first trail drives from Texas to shipping points in Kansas and later had trailed breeding stock to the northern plains. He had been bucked off, bucked over, fell on, rolled on, kicked, bit, pawed, whipped, frost-bit, sunburned, starved, ptomained, shot at, cold-cocked, blindsided, run off, run over, run out, bailed out, and thrown out. Through all of this there was but a single thing he could count on, one thing as sure as a hangover at the end of a three-month trail drive: that he would always and forever be broke.

But for a long, long time being broke didn't bother him any more than a cold-backed bronc did. He took both in an easy-going stride. He figured two things: one, if he got bucked off he would crawl back in the saddle; and two, the next payday was already on its way. For a long time this philosophy served him well. Life was just one cowtown after another. He would always be young and healthy, somebody would always make whiskey cheap enough for a cowboy to drink, the dance hall and saloon girls he paid money to for services rendered would always use enough of it to keep their faces painted and holes out of their stockings, so let the good times roll, yee-haw.

But as the years fled by, and the creases around his mouth and the crow's tracks around his eyes grew deeper, he changed. The change itself was a long time in forming. For years it hung back in the untended, barely lit corners of the brain—of which there were a multitude—growing, but very slowly.

Until the spring of 1879. Until a four-year-old roan blew up one cold morning while Jesse was dragging calves to the branding fire. The rope was tied hard and fast to the saddle horn. Just as a small calf was roped something spooked the bronc—had it been a heavier calf on the other end of the rope the bronc might not have bucked so high or so hard. But it wasn't and he did. That old bronc was "chinning the moon," but two kinds of cold iron were getting the best of him: the Coldiron on top of him, and the cold iron of Jesse's rowels in his ribs.

Cowboy, bronc, and choking, bouncing calf went over the top of the branding fire scattering wood, fire, hot irons, and hurrahing men. It was one "helluva storm." The frightened, insane horse went high into the air, sunned his navel and failed to get his feet under him before his falling half-ton of squealing muscle and bone slammed into the frost-hard ground flat on his side, Jesse's spurs still in his belly. After the dust settled, after the bronc kicked and flounced and got his feet underneath him and ran off, after Jesse crawled away, it was seen that he would need a new pair of boots come payday because the right one of the pair he was wearing was ruined by the bloody, jagged bone sticking through it.

He was laid up until fall. The infection that set in was conquered only by, as the wagon cook put it, "more guts than ere any Chicago butcher seed."

After the infection relinquished the fight to the lean cowboy the foot began to heal. By September, it could support Jesse's one hundred and seventy pounds in a limping walk on soft ground. By mid-October, it could be pressed against the curved bottom of an oak, oxbowed stirrup without unbearable pain. By November, it was healed as much as it ever would be, which was enough that its owner was able to forget it, having already learned to live with the dull pain that came after several hours in the saddle.

After twenty-five years of punching cows Jesse had been forced into an extended period of idleness. Physically, he might not have been able to ride, but mentally he rode a lot of back trails, prowled through a lot of virgin thoughts and tried to find a pass high enough for him to peek over and get a glimpse of the trail that led through the wilderness that was the future. At that, of course, he failed. He learned only what so many others before him had learned: The past stretches out behind you clear and flat, and is as easy to read as a trail herd in six inches of fresh snow; but the trail ahead disappears into a dark, rocky, unexplored wilderness.

When he had been eighteen years old the future had beckoned to him as a seductress, revealing only enough of herself to make him want to see more, offering glimpses of thrills and adventure but never letting him see all he wanted. After a pair of decades had slid underneath his stirrups, that seductress had lost much of her former charm. Not all of it by any means, but she was now approached with less passion than in earlier years, and with a great deal more prudence.

Jesse was smart enough to know that it was only luck that had stopped the infection before it forced amputation of his foot, maybe the whole leg, and put a sudden stop to his cowboying. What, he couldn't help but wonder, would become of him if something like that did happen? The knowledge of the certain spills, wrecks, and dangers of all kinds that rode with all men who lived his kind of life held no more fear for him than they ever had. But what if he couldn't cowboy for a living? It was all he knew how to do, all he wanted to do. He had seen it happen to others, no better or no worse than himself and, in most cases, the eventual outcome was not pretty. Usually, odd jobs and then handouts plus a good sprinkling of self-pity, led to a few years of drunkenness—brought to an end, at last, by one-too-many nights in an open alley, or by the trembling grasp of once-strong and proud hands around the cold butt of a brain-pointed Colt or Smith and Wesson.

Somewhere toward the end of his convalescence, all of this wondering and thinking combined into the realization that before his trail broke and fell into six feet of cold clay, he wanted to be able to look at the world and say: "I work for no man but Jesse Coldiron. I may not have much, but what I've got was earned through blood, sweat, and saddle sores and it's just as important to me as all the stacks of gold in the world."

Jesse Coldiron's mind was made up. His thoughts and energy were focused on one thing and one thing only: to have his own cattle. On cowboy wages that was a mighty awesome undertaking. But his resolve was strong, so strong that at times *he* was more surprised than anyone. He gave up things that he had once considered as outright necessities—painted women, gambling, and cheap whiskey.

For five years—five long years—the only luxury Jesse Coldiron allowed himself was smoking tobacco. He bought clothes only when the rags he was wearing would no longer keep him covered or warm. Boots that he normally would have thrown away he mended himself. He avoided barbershop haircuts and shaves like he would have avoided the plague. On the rare occasions when he did venture into a cowtown for ranch supplies or for his own bare necessities, he didn't dare look into a saloon or dance hall, and once his business was completed he left town like Lot must have left Sodom.

It wasn't easy; he dearly missed his vices as any carefree cowboy would. Only now he wasn't exactly carefree. Now he had a goal, a mission, a quest. Slowly, very slowly, agonizingly so, his money pile began to grow.

There also grew within his angular frame a restlessness that he could not explain. It was caused in part, he guessed, because he wanted his own cattle so much. It was also the result of swift changes that were taking place across the West; changes that he could not stop; changes that he could not have dreamed of earlier—towns and cities springing up out of nothing, barbed-wire fences, railroads, telegraph lines, and a relentless surge of people from the East each wanting their piece of cheap land in the golden West.

But on top of all of this, something further added to Jesse's restlessness. Something that he could not put his finger on. Was it hives? Bile? Gas? Was it lack of whiskey? Women? In the end he gave up on trying to figure out what it was and told himself that it would pass when he had his own cattle and was his own boss.

In 1881, he had been working for a Panhandle outfit that trailed steers to Montana for fattening. When the drive was finished he stayed on the northern plains instead of accompanying his Texas friends home. He stayed for one reason—money. The going pay for a hand in Texas was $25 a month. In Montana it was $40. He hated the sub-zero winters with a frost-bit passion, but the $15 a month extra was nearly enough to pay for one cow.

Finally, he had saved $1,000. Not much to show for five years of living like a nun and working like a Turk. But enough to encourage a banker in Miles City to loan him another $800. With the $1,800 he bought a hundred head of Longhorn-Hereford crossbred two-year-old heifers from that same banker—which *might* have had something to do with his getting the loan— and even had $200 left over for expenses.

The heifers were in Colorado, and Jesse took ownership of them in April of 1884. Part of the deal was that he could graze them on the banker's range until the next spring, then he would have to be gone with them. Coldiron went for the deal like he used to go for the nearest dance hall on payday.

And now, here he was a few months later, winter not even really started, half of the expense money gone, sitting on a lonesome hill somewhere in the Panhandle with night closing in. It was snowing harder, the wind picking up momentum like a cannonball rolling down an icy slope, and the whole of his ninety-eight-head herd—Colorado cockleburrs and lightning had each already claimed one heifer—was God only knew where, with nothing to save them from another snowstorm but an out-of-humor, out-of-luck cowboy, himself three-fourths lost.

Jesse was no financial wizard, but it didn't require one to make a quick analysis of his new worth. He rubbed a hand across the thick brown mustache growing between thin lips and nose and quickly weighed his assets against his liabilities. It was no surprise that the end of the scales holding the $800 note fell to the ground with a sickening thud when balanced against a herd of lost heifers.

Dumping more tobacco into the cigarette paper, the cowboy dared the brown to toss his head again. He didn't, and the cigarette was licked and stuck into Jesse's mouth with the left hand while the right rasped a match across the hard, dry leather that holstered the heavy Colt riding on his hip. The sputtering flame was lifted to meet the cigarette and held there, protected from the wind by cupped hands.

Jesse's eyes lifted suddenly from the small flame and made a quick sweep to the south. He had heard something. A faint sound struggling against the wind.

Jesse relaxed, inhaled smoke, and waited.

When the glowing tip of the cigarette was an inch from his mustache the sound came again. It was still not strong, but strong enough that he was sure, this

CHAPTER

The saddle Jesse Coldiron straddled had been purchased second-hand by him for the princely sum of
$14.50 back in his spendthrift days. But it was a good
saddle, it bore the well-known and respected Gallatin
stamp, had an exposed double rigging, square skirts,
and even though it showed much wear and tear, it
was well-oiled and repaired and had hardly a squeak
in it. The spurs on Jesse's boot heels were not as
quiet, the hole in the center of the inch-and-a-half
rowels had become enlarged with use and age and
they jingled with a sort of merry cadence to the movement of his horse. The gear in the packsaddle on the
dun was louder than a jingle and had no particular
cadence about it; rather it was a symphony of un-
orchestrated clangs and bangs. These were the sounds
that accompanied Jesse as he trotted off the hill, but
so accustomed was he to them that he would have
sworn there was not a sound to be heard in all of that
desolate land.

After a mile Jesse topped a narrow ridge and looked

down into a draw, and there were the cattle he had heard bawling. And there was something else, something that made him want to shout his blasphemies into the air once again. There was one of those damned drift fences he had been hearing about! He knew there was some reason, besides general principles, for his cussing the big cow outfits—the Boss Ranchers he called them—but he had forgotten what it was. Now he was looking at it: A barbed wire fence that stretched both east and west as far as the waning light would allow him to see.

The cattle bunched up against the fence were not his. From where he sat on top of the ridge, in the fading light and snow flurries, it was impossible to read a brand on them, but these were straight-bred Longhorns, not crossbreeds.

He contemplated the fence momentarily, knew that it could be both good and bad for him. Good, because it would stop the further drift of his heifers. Bad, because if another storm was coming the cattle would ball-up on it and freeze or suffocate to death. At any rate, his own heifers should be along the fence somewhere and he had better find them. Making a random choice, he rode off the ridge to the west, hunkered down a little further into his overcoat, and prepared to ride the night through if need be.

Suddenly it started to snow harder, the flakes no longer soft and wet but now small and hard. They stung like deerflies whenever they struck bare skin. After covering but two hundred yards along the fence Jesse pulled up and turned in the saddle to look at the handful of scraggly cows again. They were lined up like dominos, horned heads held low and only inches from the barbed wire, bony rears turned toward the wind, waiting, Jesse knew, to die. And they would, if they spent the coming dark and cold in a driving snowstorm.

"What the hell," he muttered to himself as he rode back toward the cattle, "a few more minutes ain't going to make much difference to my cattle one way or the other." Stopping just short of the cattle, he dismounted, dug his pliers out of his saddlebags, and began clipping, saying under his breath, "To hell with this goddamn fence."

The cowboy with the sharp pliers didn't consider the drift fence to be one of the Boss Ranchers' better ideas. Oh, the idea might not have been too far out of kilter, but fences like that just never worked like they were supposed to. He didn't hold it against them for trying . . . the hell he didn't, he reconsidered as he cut another strand of wire. After all, they had all the grass in that part of Texas, from No Man's Land on the north all the way across the Llano to the south. Most of them didn't have it by legal say-so but by the say-so of influential friends—Misters Colt and Winchester. But he couldn't say that they didn't have a right to a big part of it, maybe most of it. They had had to fight outlaws and Indians ever since the first cattle set foot in the Panhandle back in the '70s. But what about the $25-a-month cowboy who did most of the work and the killing and the dying? When did he get his part of the grass bonanza?

Jesse had to give the Boss Ranchers credit for one thing: When they did something they did it in a big way. This was no piddling effort of a couple of strands of wire and a puny post every rifle-shot apart. No sir, this was a five-wire job with a stout post planted every rod. The idea of the fence was to keep northern cattle from drifting south during the winter storms and taking up residence along the protective breaks of the river. During bad winters cattle as far north as Wyoming would drift as far south as the Panhandle. The Boss Ranchers weren't eager to share their grass with their northern neighbors. But he figured the boys in South Texas didn't much cotton to the idea of pasturing Panhandle cattle that drifted into their range, either. It looked to him, if no one built a drift fence, all the cattle would drift and everyone would come out even on the deal. And that's the way everybody used to think. But times had changed.

Jesse grinned as the last wire was cut; it suddenly occurred to him why the fence wasn't working like it was supposed to—people kept cutting it.

With the wires cut and pulled back to the post on each side, all he had to do was to remount and ease around the cows and get them started through the opening. Once through, they would take care of themselves by drifting until they found shelter: they might all die before they found it, but at least they would have a chance. Pushed up against a fence during a blizzard, a big herd might have a few survivors; those in the back would keep pushing and crowding those in front until either the fence gave way or the ones in front were crushed and piled up until the rest could walk over their corpses, and over the fence in the process. But a small herd would be doomed to the last animal. A small herd like the one he now watched trot through the hole he had made—or a small herd like his own.

The weather was deteriorating by the minute, and by the time the last cow was through the hole a powdery snow was being whipped and whirled around and into everything, Jesse's face and eyes included. He knew that it had suddenly become time to stop worrying about this cattle, any cattle, and start worrying about himself. In another half-hour it would be pitch dark, and the dark of a night blizzard is one of the most frightening and dangerous things a lone man on the open prairie could run up against.

Things had closed down so rapidly around Jesse, with the night and the snow, he could see only a hundred yards. It was at that limit that he first saw an approaching form, dark against the whitening ground, but also fuzzy and indistinguishable. Leaning forward in the saddle and straining his eyes, he saw the coming apparition to be a horse and rider. Jug saw them, too, and stood still, head up, eyes big, nostrils flared.

Jesse quickly weighed the situation. He had been up many trails in his nearly forty years, and if he had learned one lesson it was not to take anything for granted. In this situation, on this night, him sitting in front of a hole he had illegally cut in the fence, an unknown rider approaching—nothing should be taken for granted. He slid his Winchester out of the boot under his right leg, levered a shell into the chamber and let the barrel rest across his left forearm.

The first thing Jesse could tell was that the man was riding a buckskin in an easy trot along the fence, coming out of the west and riding right for him. After a few more steps Jesse saw the rifle in the man's right hand, but its muzzle was in the air and its butt was resting on his thigh. The man's left hand held the saddle horn and the reins. He was leaning over slightly, his weight all in his stirrups. Jug nickered a soft greeting, his ears straight forward.

The man and the buckskin came on at an even pace, the man not looking up from the ground in front of him. When they had closed to thirty yards, the buckskin stopped, threw up his head and returned Jug's greeting. With a surprise the man looked at

Jesse and threw the rifle to his shoulder. With no time to wonder about what was happening, Jesse brought his own carbine up. The sharp crack, the fire leaping out of the other rifle told him he was an instant too late. He had heard the unmistakable sound of soft lead striking softer flesh many times in his life, but never before had he provided the flesh to make the familiar "whump" sound. Before he had any sensation at all, he knew he had been shot. He saw the bright muzzle-flash of the other rifle and felt the bullet tear into him all in the same split second. For an instant the earth seemed to stop: The snowflakes descended no farther, the flame licking out of the rifle froze. Then the world was put in motion again and Jesse felt something try to jerk him from the saddle by his left arm. This was followed by a searing pain that raked his left side. In a daze, his mind contemplated whether this was where he would die; but if it was, why?

Of all the tight scrapes he had been in over the years and across the miles, this was the tightest. But it was not the first, and he didn't panic. He realized with a strange calmness that the most dangerous threat to his life was not the bullet that had already found his body, but the next one that would come if he let the man get off another shot from thirty yards. Brushing pain and fear aside, he brought up his rifle and fired, not even taking time to aim. The instant he squeezed the trigger he knew he had been lucky. His 200 grains of soft lead caught the stranger full in the chest, hurling him backwards. The frightened buckskin whirled at the shot and kicked over the limp body that tumbled to the ground at his hind feet.

Jesse kept the stranger in his sights for thirty seconds after he rolled to the ground. The horses snorted their uneasiness at the sudden flurry of commotion, the rapid exchange of gunfire, the smell of blood, and the unfamiliar gurgling sounds coming from the man stretched faceup on the snow-dusted sage.

Jesse coaxed Jug closer to the prone figure. A big circle of red was already soaking through his heavy coat. The gurgling sounds were still coming from his chest, but they were more shallow now, and rapid. Jesse knew the man was lung-shot, drowning in his own blood.

"Who the hell are you?" Jesse asked from the saddle, his voice not strong. All he received for his effort was a dying gasp. Dismounting, he stepped closer, but when he saw the set eyes he knew the man was dead.

The stranger was now beyond caring, but Jesse cared. He cared a great deal. He wanted to live! Blood from his wound was trickling down his side and into his britches. He knew no vital organ had been hit—the wound was too high in the shoulder. And since he still had some use of the arm he knew no bones had been shattered. Still, it was a bad wound. Any wound in a snowstorm could be fatal. Maybe it was only because he was feeling lonely and mortal but the storm seemed to have grown in intensity even since the shooting. He knew that if he had to spend the night without shelter, the wind and the snow and the cold would devour him as a pack of gaunt lobo wolves would devour a newborn calf.

He put the rifle in its scabbard, forced everything from his mind except surviving, and with much difficulty, climbed into the saddle. The loss of blood was making him weak and light-headed—soon it would render him unconscious.

The loose buckskin was trotting off, toward the

east and along the fence, like he knew where he wanted to go. Jesse decided quickly that his best bet, maybe his only bet, was to let Jug follow him. He wrapped the bridle reins around the saddle horn, gave the brown his head, and told himself that no matter what, he had to stay in the saddle.

In a short while he lost all sense of time. He rode on and on through the blinding snow, Jug's nose only inches from the buckskin's tail, the dun packhorse following Jug. In Jesse's spinning, semiconscious mind, they remained locked in that formation. The only reality he knew was that of a wounded man riding a big brown horse, following a riderless buckskin into a snowy, frozen, dark eternity. And then there was no reality at all. There was nothing.

CHAPTER

3

The earth ground out the next two days, the twenty-first and twenty-second of November, without the knowledge of Jesse Coldiron. Both days were raw, cold, and miserable. The first was whited-out by a powdery, wind-driven snow, bouncing off bare ground and piling deep on the south side of everything from bear grass to steep banks to frozen carcasses. The second opened as the first had closed, but by midday knew decreasing snowfall and slackening wind, and by nightfall, blinking stars and bitter-cold stillness.

During the night following that second day, shafts of consciousness began penetrating Jesse's mind, coming and going, intermixing with so many different images that it was impossible to separate the real from the unreal. One moment he would feel the terrible burning of a bullet eating its way into his body; then he would see the hides of his heifers hanging on a barbed-wire fence and flapping in the wind like drying sheets; or he would be driving a thousand head of Longhorn-Hereford crossbred cattle into his Colorado canyon, all fat and slick; another time he would smell a woman's sweet hair and feel a tender hand upon him, then his own body as it decayed underneath a snowdrift.

Sometime in the afternoon of the third day he finally forced open his heavy eyelids. They did not try once and give up their labor for another hour, as had been the routine earlier. Instead, they tried again and again until they stayed open. But it did no good, for his eyes would not focus on anything.

Jesse squeezed his eyelids closed and held them that way for a few seconds hoping that when they were reopened things would be bright and clear. They were not. Only when he tried to sit up and the shooting pain in his shoulder hit him like a strong whiff of smelling salts did his head clear and his brown eyes relay sensible messages.

Pain forced him on his back again. He risked raising his head to study the small room. On the wall toward his feet sunshine streamed through a small window, and beside the window was the only door. All the walls were adobe and the floor was packed earth. On the opposite wall was a rock fireplace with a heaping pile of ashes and red coals. The bunk he lay on was nothing more than a few dirty blankets spread over a row of rough slats. The whole works was encompassed by a rickety framework of splintery two-by-fours.

As much as he knew the shoulder would hurt, Jesse was determined to get off his back. Setting his teeth, he swung his feet to the floor. The pain was bad, but not as bad as he had imagined. Only when he was sitting on the edge of the bunk did he realize that someone had removed his shirt and the top half of his long handles. A blood-soaked bandage covered his wound.

He stood, wavering like a drunk before catching his balance, and then ran a hand along his face feeling five days' growth of whiskers. He looked the room over again, searching for the rest of his clothes, his boots, his gunbelt. He didn't see them, and there was nothing to hide them but a crude wooden table and three cowhide-bottomed chairs.

The cowboy's usually stout muscles had to muster all their strength to move his gaunt form to the window. His eyes recoiled quickly from the bright snow outside. Finally, they adjusted and he saw a picket corral and rock barn a hundred feet to the southeast. Jug and his dun were in the corral along with a bay and a paint, all four munching brown prairie hay that filled a manger next to the barn. The horses stopped chewing, raised their heads and looked toward the west.

Jesse saw at a glance what had drawn their attention —two other horses were coming down the long slope that carried the drift fence westward. On the lead horse was a man; in tow was a buckskin. Across the saddle of the buckskin was a dead man.

Jesse knew the buckskin, and he knew where its cargo had come from.

He was sitting on the edge of the bed again when the door opened and a small man stepped inside the room, stomped the snow off his boots and pulled off his hat. Out of the hat two feet of the blackest, thickest hair fell down the man's shoulders! *He,* quite obviously, was not a man.

The woman kept her eyes downcast. If the long black hair had first drawn Jesse's eyes and made him momentarily forget his shoulder, it was nothing compared to the moment her arms went backward and her chest forward as she removed her coat. Under other, more ordinary circumstances, the curved butt of a big Remington revolver sticking out of a waistband might have drawn his undivided attention. But Jesse had not known an ordinary circumstance since the first snows had fallen on his heifers in the Colorado foothills. It wasn't that he didn't notice the Remington, it was just that its cold steel could not magnetize his brown eyes like the bulge of warm, full breasts straining against a corduroy shirt.

She was thin and tired-looking, but pretty; and the sudden transfiguration of her from man to woman held the cowboy in a trance as he studied her tan, smooth skin, and dark features.

The silence and stillness that filled the little room was broken when she lifted her eyes and saw him sitting on the edge of the bunk. With a frightened, startled expression she jerked the big revolver from her waistband, leveled it at him and without hesitation employed both thumbs to draw its hammer to full cock.

"You . . ." she started.

"Whoa now!" Jesse exclaimed.

The muzzle of the Remington did not waver, nor did the dark eyes behind it. The woman's handsome face was as expressionless as a big-eyed prairie owl's.

Jesse kept his seat, held up both hands chest-high with the palms turned toward the woman as a show that he meant no harm to her. "Hold on a minute, ma'am," he said in a calmer voice. "What's going on around here? Don't you folks believe in letting a man talk?"

Her words were smooth, yet laced with bitterness:

"I guess you gave Ward a chance to talk before you killed him. Is that right?"

"No . . . I mean . . . look, ma'am, just let me talk. Was Ward the man I . . ."

"That's right," she said, cold and sharp as any timberline axe, "Ward James was the man you killed. And I already know what happened! When his horse came in without him with blood on the saddle, I knew I would find him dead . . . and I did, this morning. I should have let you die, right out there in front of the barn where you fell off in the blizzard, but I had to be sure—and now I am."

Across the fifteen feet that separated them, Jesse could see tears filling her dark eyes. "Lady," he said in a voice and manner meant to appease, "I'm sorry about him, but he just rode up from nowhere and shot me. Yeah, I shot him but I didn't have any choice because he was trying to kill me. I guess I was just luckier than he was."

The woman blinked back the tears. Her voice became steadier than ever. "You're a liar! Ward would never do that! I guess he cut the hole in the fence too. The fence that he was paid to keep repaired."

"No," Jesse reluctantly admitted, aware of the damage it would do his case. "I cut the fence. But only to keep a few old cows from standing right there against it until they died. Soon as I got it cut and the cows drove through this man just comes up outa the dark and the next thing I know is that I'm fighting for my life."

"Save your breath," she said with both hands still on the butt of the gun, its muzzle now dipping and pointing at the floor somewhere between them. "I know Ward better than that; after all these years I should. He must have caught you stealing cattle, or

27

maybe you're a hired gunfighter, bought and paid for by the troublemakers around Hogtown. Whatever you are, whoever you are, you're going to pay for what you've done."

Closing the door behind her with one foot, she took three steps into the room and stopped at the table. She sat in a cowhide-bottomed chair, still keeping her two-handed grip on the weapon but letting the butt rest on the unfinished table top.

"What are you going to do now, ma'am?"

"I'm going to kill you if you force me to. If not, I'm taking you to Tascosa so the law can hang you."

"Look, Mrs., uh, James—it was an awful thing that happened, I'll agree to that sure enough, but what's a man supposed to do? I mean, he just rode up and shot me. I just threw up my rifle and shot back. Didn't even take time to aim because he had already leveled down on me again. Don't ask me why; we didn't take time to socialize much. All I had time for was one quick shot, done in self-defense. Now, if that's a crime . . ."

"You liar," she retorted, losing control. "You liar! Ward was not that kind of a . . ." She composed herself again, said with great assurance, "No jury will believe that story—not with two bullets in Ward."

Jesse straightened. "What?"

She didn't answer.

"What was that about two bullets?" he asked again.

The woman looked at him but said nothing. Jesse fingered his bandage, looking at the floor and thinking.

After a moment Jesse said softly, "Mrs. James, I'm going to get up and go out that door."

At that statement, she came back from wherever it was that her mind had taken her. Jesse saw her hands tighten on the Remington.

"I'm not going to try to run away," he affirmed. "I'm just going out to the barn in my stocking feet. I've got to see something out there. Now you can either shoot me right now or bring the gun and follow me."

It was a gamble. Jesse was convinced of the woman's honest—if mistaken—appraisal of what had happened. Just as he was convinced that she was not bluffing about using the gun if she had to. But in spite of all of that, he didn't think her capable of shooting an unarmed, barefoot, wobbly-kneed cowboy who was not threatening her.

Coldiron moved slowly to the door, out of deference to the lady with the gun as well as his own unsteady balance. As he skirted the table he heard her chair scoot back and when he stepped outside he knew she was not far behind.

By the second step outside, he had to stop and allow his eyes to adjust to the intense glare of the clean snow. Once he was able to see something other than colored spots he stepped on toward the barn, surveying his surroundings as he walked. A wide, sandy creek lay a hundred yards to the east of the barn, while to the north, just behind the shack, was a tall caliche bluff. Jesse recognized the place as an old sheep camp but now, obviously, a line camp used to watch the drift fence, or at least a portion of it.

"Mind telling me what day this is, Mrs. James?" Jesse asked over a shoulder.

After a few seconds came the reply, "Thursday."

"Thursday?" Jesse repeated to himself, trying to comprehend how long he had lain unconscious. No wonder he felt weak, he thought. And no telling where the hell his heifers were. Or whether they were still alive.

The buckskin was tied inside the barn, the body still across the saddle. Jesse unceremoniously untied the corpse and dragged it down. With no thought about the effect upon the woman, he then used a knee and his strong right arm to overcome the stiffening effects of cold and death, forcing the body flat upon the earthen barn floor. Jesse unbuttoned the man's coat and ripped off the shirt buttons, exposing the pallid, naked chest.

Two bullet wounds, just like the woman had said. One was high in the chest in a mat of curly black hair that was slicked down with frozen blood. The other was lower, in the stomach, about two inches right of the navel.

Jesse continued kneeling by the body, studying the wounds and thinking, until he heard the woman sobbing quietly. He then found a yellow slicker hanging on a nail and covered the corpse with it.

Seeing his gear thrown in a corner beside the door, Jesse said, "If you'll get my rifle over there, there's something I'd like to show you."

After a few seconds of looking at the covered body, the woman went to the saddle and pulled the rifle out with one hand, still pointing the Remington at the cowboy with the other.

"Now," instructed Jesse, "work the lever until all the shells have ejected."

It was hard to manage holding the rifle and working the lever while keeping the revolver trained on the stranger, but in a few seconds the Winchester coughed up no more brass and lead.

"Now count the shells, Mrs. James."

She did so reluctantly, with the toe of her boot and said, "Eleven."

Pointing at the saddle on the buckskin, Jesse said:

"I see you picked up his rifle. I'd sure like for you to get it and do the same thing."

"Now look here . . ."

"Please, ma'am, just do it. Then you can stand me up against the wall and shoot me if you want to."

With a haggard, disgusted countenance, she performed the same chore on the other rifle. "Seven," she said. "Now are you satisfied?"

"Like I figured," Jesse said, more to himself than to her. Then he added, "Mrs. James, if you'll think about it for a minute, you'll see that Ward must've already had a shooting scrap before we bumped into each other along the fence."

"I don't see any . . ."

"Mrs. James," he interrupted—he was tired and impatient with her for not seeing what, to him, was obvious—"his rifle is the same as mine. Same make and same model, a '73 Winchester carbine. They both hold twelve rounds when full. Any cowboy will tell you that everybody carries their guns loaded to the hilt because cartridges are easier to carry in the magazine than anywhere else.

"So it's plain to see, since he was shot twice and only one shell has been fired from my rifle, someone else shot him, too. And he shot at them, that's what accounts for his rifle only having seven rounds in it. He shot five times, once at me and four times at somebody else. Don't you see? He'd already taken a slug, more'n likely the one in the belly, before he saw me. He was probably trying to get back here. Prob'ly half outa his head with pain, and when he saw me he fired out of instinct. And I had to shoot back or die.

"The truth of the matter is, Mrs. James, I shot your husband. But all I did was put him outa his misery. Whoever shot him the first time is the one that killed him. You said I was prob'ly a cattle thief or a hired gun, but I'm a long ways from either. All I am is a cowboy come down here to get my lost cattle. They're all I've got to show for a lifetime of punching cows. My heifers drifted down here during the first snowstorm. What happened between me and your man was all an accident. I didn't come here to shoot anybody or to get shot. But sometimes we don't have much say-so over what happens to us.''

Suddenly the woman seemed to be drained of everything, and Jesse thought she might collapse. Not only did the blood rush from her face, but with it all her anger and her grief. She lowered the revolver, stood motionless for half a minute, then walked out of the barn.

Jesse fingered the dried blood on his bandage again and watched as she neared the house. He realized his rough ways—how he had manhandled the body and his callous description of Ward James's dying—had caused her even greater pain. Hell, he hadn't meant to hurt her. He hadn't intended the things he had done and said to look and sound the way they did. Whatever twenty-five years of cowboying gave a man, the gentle way to handle things was not included in the package.

CHAPTER

4

A cold morning sun was straining to rise above the great, white expanse of the Texas Panhandle. The first golden rays of the day were just touching the trees along Rito Blanco Creek and the top of the rock barn at the line camp along its west bank. No breeze stirred the nearly leafless treetops or moved the dried sunflowers between the camp and the sandy creek. The sparrows that were lined up along the ridge of the barn did their customary quarreling, paying no mind to the cowboy in the corral below, or to the horse he was trying to catch.

Jesse led Jug into the barn and began saddling him. As the saddle settled on the brown back, he saw the James woman leave the house and walk toward the barn. She was quite a woman. He chuckled to himself—she was easy to look at, even without having the advantage of a few straight shots of hundred-proof whiskey. Ward James must have been some man, at least a lucky man. Then he remembered the slicker-shrouded corpse a few paces away and reconsidered. Anyway, not many cowpunchers had a woman who looked like her.

As she walked through the barn door Jesse realized that he was no longer just watching her, he was staring. He shifted his attention back to the saddle, leaned over, reached under Jug's belly and grabbed the front cinch.

The woman entered the barn and crossed the thirty feet of space separating them. "I don't know who you are," she said to the cowboy on the other side of the horse.

Jesse didn't look up. "Jesse Coldiron."

She walked around the rear of the horse and watched as he stepped into his chaps. "Where are you going?" she asked in a demanding tone. Then before Jesse could answer she added, "I didn't think you'd be well enough to ride yet." Jesse knew that was the truth—as long as she thought him too weak to ride, she didn't need to worry about him leaving, and her only concern had been to protect herself. He could see the Remington bulging beneath her coat.

He knew she had been through a long night. Still, she didn't look as bad as she had yesterday afternoon when he examined Ward's body. She was no longer as wan as before.

"Reckon I better ride whether I feel like it or not, ma'am," he said as he buckled his chaps. "I've got my heifers to find, it's been three days since . . . well, since the shooting. And it was two days before that when I last seen 'em. But first, I'm riding up the fence a ways past where me and Ward met up. I just want to see what might be there. Maybe I'll find some sign of my cattle or some clues as to exactly what happened to your husband."

"And then?" she asked, her voice caustic.

"And then I'll come back here and take you and Ward's body to wherever you need to go. . . . Or, I'll bury him here for you."

"I want to take him to Tascosa." She stiffened and added, "Where the sheriff is."

"Okay," Jesse said and let it drop there, pretending not to notice the subtle challenge. She was right, though, about talking to the sheriff. If it had been just him and the dead man, Jesse would have buried the man and been about finding his cattle. But the woman made a difference. If he didn't talk to the law, he could find his picture on the walls of every sheriff's office in the country.

Jesse gathered up the reins and started leading Jug toward the door. The woman followed him.

The cowboy went on out the door, not exactly at a brisk pace and not much like a man eagerly anticipating his day's chores.

"How do I know you'll be back?" she asked.

He stopped, put his left foot in the stirrup and said without looking at her, "You don't."

He slung his right leg over the cantle of the saddle, wincing from the shooting pain in his shoulder, and said, "Maybe I'm lying about the shooting. Could be I'll never be back." Then settling into the cold saddle seat, he looked down at her. "Or maybe I'll be back because I said I would."

She stood in the cold shadow of the barn, wondering what kind of a man he really was. She felt the heavy Remington tugging at the waistband of her britches, but she did not reach for it. She wished she had the stomach to pull it out, cock it, look down its long barrel and put a bullet between Jesse Coldiron's broad shoulders. But she knew she could not. If he were coming at her, maybe; but not with him riding away, and she hated herself for being so weak. Maybe she was watching Ward's killer ride out, not lifting a finger to stop him.

Jug was a big horse, weighing twelve hundred pounds, and like many horses that size, he was rough. The man on his back had told him many times in the past how rough he trotted, but never had Jug's feet jarred the ground any harder than they did on that morning when Jesse's shoulder was just beginning to heal. Before the first mile had been negotiated the gelding had been on the receiving end of no less than three good Coldiron cussings. Jesse's temper was not helped any by having spent the night sleeping on the floor of the barn, or having only jerky and coffee for supper and again for breakfast.

After they had trotted a couple of miles the sun was high enough and warm enough to continue the thaw that had begun the day before. Jug carried Jesse over rolling hills, through the increasing mush, across wide, sage-covered draws, and down narrow gullies murmuring with the soft sound of busy rivulets of ice-cold water.

They rode past cattle that had drifted against the fence during the storm and died. In one draw alone, he counted over two hundred head.

At each dead animal, or pile of animals, Jesse checked to make sure they were not his. By the time he reached the place where he had cut the hole in the fence he had seen several hundred dead cows, calves, yearlings, bulls, and aged steers, but none were wearing his brand or his earmark.

Jesse made a scouring search for hundreds of yards in every direction from the spot of his deadly encounter with Ward James. All he found was melting snow.

In an hour he was riding west along the fence

again. Another three miles brought him to a rise over-looking a wide draw. He pulled up Jug's head and stopped short. Below him were more dead cattle, maybe twenty or thirty head, but even from four hundred yards these cattle put a knot in his stomach. He could tell they were his, even though their bodies were just beginning to be visible. The sun's warming rays had melted enough of the snow covering them to reveal the soft brownish red hair and white face characteristic of Longhorn-Hereford cattle.

He was right. The first stiff carcass he rode up to had his Bar C drying in the bright sun. In all, there were twenty-five head lying along a short stretch of fence. Jesse carefully checked the brand on each. Not a one lacked a Bar C.

Jesse dismounted and sat on one of the heifers. He pushed his hat back, scratched his pale forehead and quickly figured that it had taken him something like a year and a half to save the money to buy the twenty-five head. Then he realized that he was lucky *all* his cattle weren't here.

Then he saw why they were not. He had been so busy looking at brands and counting dead cattle he had not seen the lifesaving hole just a few yards down the fence. The way the wires were pulled back and not wadded and twisted, it was almost certain that someone had cut the fence and let the rest of the heifers drift with the storm. There was a good chance then that he still had seventy-three head alive and safe, maybe somewhere along the Canadian River.

The slim cowboy mounted, pulled his hat down, and looked at the cattle again. "Damn, Jug," he muttered, "there's eighteen months of hard work lying there. . . . I hope the buzzards and the coyotes appreciate all the trouble I went to, to bring 'em this beef. . . . No, by God I don't either. I hope they eat so much they all die of the founder."

Jesse had an impulse to head south, right then, and see about the rest of his cattle—and to hell with anything else. But he knew he couldn't. He had to get the shooting cleared up and be sure the law in Tascosa got the right version of how it happened. And then there was Mrs. James. However unwillingly, he had been partly responsible for her reaching widowhood so young. That being the case, what a man ought to do was take her and her husband's body to Tascosa.

Some things just seem to build their own momentum, no matter what. Death seemed to be dogging Jesse Coldiron now, and everywhere he turned there was that ghastly, blank stare. He had seen it on the face of Ward James and on hundreds of cattle, and he sensed he wasn't through seeing it yet.

He spied a dark, curving object sticking up through the snow and resting against the bottom wire of the fence. It was a man's coated arm. Jesse dug the body out from under a snowdrift and found a man of about forty with two bullet wounds. One was in his upper right leg and another, in the throat, had severed the man's jugular vein and paled his skin to match the color of the snow.

While Jesse undertook the grisly task of scraping snow from a dead man, another man, many miles to the southeast, was no less perturbed at the way events had unrolled for him that day. The man was leaning against a post that supported the porch roof in front of a cowtown cafe; he wore a scowl on his hard-looking face, and watched the street in front of him like a hawk. He was not particularly surprised to see the tall, thin horsebacker coming up the street toward him. Some days, that man got under his skin deeper than a needle-sharp corral splinter.

The man on the horse stopped before the cafe, pushed back his hat and grinned. "I could be damn wrong," he said, "but I'd wager a couple of drinks of Hogtown whiskey that yore gal friend ain't in her little nest yet."

The big man on the porch straightened, pulled his hat down over his eyes, and angrily bit the end off a long cigar. The tall horsebacker was loving it. "You don't reckon," he jabbed, "that she's scratching around in a new chicken yard, do ya?"

The man on the porch looked out from under the brim of his hat with eyes that could singe. "Goddamn you, Slim, what me or her do is none of your business. I can promise you one thing though, she'll never scratch in anybody's yard but mine, and she knows it."

With those words he stepped off the porch, untied his horse at the hitching post, and stepped into the saddle. With the same malevolent threat in his eyes, he looked at the other man again and said: "Did you have the boys put the new cattle where I said?"

"Yeah," Slim replied, "just like you said. By God, one more snowstorm like that and we can retire. Say, you heard any talk around town about anybody finding them dead fellers?"

"No. You better be damn sure that cowboy don't show up somewhere alive and calling names."

"Ain't no way, boss. No way. He got off a couple of shots, but then I hit him square in the boiler room. Like I said, I couldn't see who the bastard was in the snow an' all, but I know he couldn't have gone more'n a hundred yards before he fell off. He's pro'bly still under a snowbank somewhere just like Bill is. No, just as shore as he kilt Bill, I kilt him. When they find one, they'll find 'em both and figure they kilt each other. . . . So all you got to fret over is who's scratching Tracey and where it is she's itching.''

Slim started to laugh, but then thought otherwise. When at last his boss quit staring at him, jerked the cigar out of his mouth, and rode away, he heaved a silent sigh of relief.

That morning, as Jesse had ridden away from the line shack, the sun had thrown long shadows toward the west. Now, as he returned, they lay in the opposite direction. Man and horse cast a long dark shape across the house and barn as he eased Jug down the slope that ended almost at the threshold of the adobe shack. The door opened and the James woman silently watched him ride into the barn. The body he had dug out of the snowbank was awkwardly draped over his saddle, and just as soon as Jug entered the barn, he let it drop to the floor.

He was tired and sore, and his shoulder throbbed. He had ridden twenty-five or thirty miles that day, half of that at a slow gait, trying to keep the body from sliding off the saddle.

Jesse stepped to the ground and stood still for a few seconds while the blood began circulating again through his aching left foot. As he was unsaddling, he saw the woman come into the barn. She leaned against a brace post and looked at the newest dead man in silence.

Jesse went about his chores, telling her what he had seen during his absence. She listened, but asked nothing and offered nothing. When he finished she turned and walked toward the open barn door. She stopped just before reaching it and turned back to the cowboy. "I didn't think you would come back."

Jesse grinned. "For a while out there I wasn't sure myself."

The woman's dark features merged with the gathering evening shadows. The huge orange sun had all but disappeared behind the hills to the southwest. The evening was still and cold, like a clear pool of spring water. As the James woman went into the shack, a coyote howl, lonely and distant, drifted over the snow-patched hills. A howl every bit as lonely and distant, thought Jesse, as that woman.

Somewhere, Jesse found the spirit to shave his week-old whiskers. And, cold as the horse trough was, he gave himself a splash bath. After he had finished he sat on a bale of hay, rolled a cigarette and thought about making a fire. He was thinking how good a strong cup of coffee would taste when his thoughts were interrupted by a soft, even voice behind him.

"I thought you'd probably need to eat something." It was the James woman, holding a tin plate filled with beans and beef in one hand and a steaming cup of coffee in the other.

Jesse raised his tired frame, stamped out the cigarette with his boot, and took the plate and cup from her. "Why, much obliged, ma'am," he said, not trying to hide his surprise.

He sat back down on the hay, placed the plate in his lap and started devouring the food. He had expected the woman to leave when he took the plate, but after a half-dozen bites she was still standing beside him. He interrupted his eating, looked up at her, and said with a nod, "I never did thank you for patching me up neither, ma'am. Guess I mighta not made it if'n you hadn't pulled me in that night.''

The woman accepted his gratitude with the same silence she had accepted his thanks for the food. Jesse looked at the plate and took another small bite. In his mind he could still see her standing silent, hands together in front of her, coal black hair pulled back from her slender face and tied with a string at her neck and again at her shoulders, wearing faded denim britches and a tan corduroy shirt, its long tail hanging out. The longer the silence went on, the more ill at ease he became. After two more bites he said without looking at her, ''I guess you got more family around Tascosa, eh?''

''No,'' she answered flatly, ''he was all the family I had left.''

The silence returned and the next time Jesse glanced toward her, her small form was walking out of the barn.

CHAPTER 5

Midmorning the next day, Saturday, the twenty-fifth of November, found most of the snow gone, save for the deepest drifts. These helplessly awaited the bright fall sun and stiff southwesterly breeze that had already claimed their less capacious counterparts.

Midmorning also found five horses strung out, bearing south and east, toward the Canadian River and the little cowtown of Tascosa. One of these horses carried a packsaddle loaded with supplies. Two others carried dead men, cold and wrapped in blankets. The remaining two horses carried a leathery-faced, thin-lipped cowboy and a small woman dressed like a man; both riders were alive but every bit as silent as the dead bodies they escorted.

The going was not particularly difficult and the hours and miles fell behind them. All morning they crossed rolling, sandy hills, cut here and there by usually dry creeks alive now with thin streams of melted snow. As morning passed into afternoon and the distance between themselves and the river narrowed, they could see the rougher terrain on the other side of the Canadian. The steep canyons, vertical-walled creeks and red and gray erosion areas grew closer and less hazy as they neared town.

When they topped a low sandy hill and saw the trees of Tascosa only two miles distant, the woman urged her mount beside the big brown gelding.

"Mr. Coldiron," she said, "I guess you should know that Ward was not my husband."

Jesse reined up. He looked at her, "But you said . . ."

"No," she corrected, "you said, and I didn't bother to tell you different. I thought it better to let you think Ward and I were married."

"I see," nodded Jesse. And in his mind he did see. He had seen it many times. A man brings a girl, usually from a saloon or dance hall, to stay with him while he is at a lonely line camp. A lot of times she didn't even have to be paid; she would come just to get out of town for a few days—and nights. Jesse was familiar with such arrangements, but he sure didn't have Mrs. James—or whatever her name was—pictured to be that kind.

"No," the woman corrected for the second time, shaking her head, "you don't see anything. It wasn't like that between Ward and me."

Jesse felt his face flush, surprised and embarrassed that she had read his thoughts. "Oh," he said. Then, "Well, it's none of my business what you an' him were . . ."

"Mr. Coldiron," she said, with the faintest hint of a smile. It was hard to see but there nonetheless, like the tiniest of stars that must be looked at sideways to be seen at all, "My name is Tracey James. Ward was my brother. I had just gotten to the line shack to visit with him when the storm hit. I work at the North Star

Cafe and live by myself in a room in back of it. And you're right—it *is* none of your business.''

Saturday afternoon in Tascosa, County Seat of Oldham County, was always a busy time. The streets were alive with pedestrians as well as with horses, buggies, and buckboards. People were going into or coming out of the saloons and businesses along Main Street or lounging on the verandas that fronted most of them. It looked like everybody was outdoors enjoying the pleasant weather they had been blessed with since the terrible blizzard the first part of the week.

Nothing much of consequence had happened all afternoon. Surely nothing important enough to draw the attention of more than a mere handful of people at one time. But now, something was sweeping over the little hamlet like a slow-moving wave. It started on the west side of town and moved eastward about as fast as a walking horse. About as fast as five walking horses, to be exact.

One at a time, or in small groups, people stopped whatever they were doing and looked. Five horses had come out of a thick growth of cottonwoods, crossed the hundred yards that separated Tascosa Creek from the town, and were now past the point where the narrow wagon road widened to become the town's Main Street.

As the horses walked past, people talked in hushed tones, many covered their mouths with their hands. They exchanged speculations with those nearest them regarding the identity of the bodies wrapped in blankets and tied across saddle seats, who the mustached cowboy was and what the pretty girl who worked at the North Star Cafe was doing with him.

"What'n hell d'ya make of that?" asked a man to the three other men around him.

No one spoke until the last of the five horses had passed, then one man pushed back his hat and drawled, "Well, I don't know what to make of the rest of it, but it looks to me like that James gal has herself a new feller." At that they all laughed.

"I wonder who he is?"

"Beats the cob outa me, but looky over yonder 'cross the street, in front of Rhinehart's store. Cain's face is getting redder'n a July plum."

"I'll lay odds he finds out who he is."

"Yeah, an' damned quick, too."

"If that feller ain't careful, he'll be riding that big brown like them other two fellers are riding their horses—slung over the saddle. Who d'ya reckon they are?"

"That feller's got guts, I'll say that—I mean, bringing them two bodies right into town."

"Yeah, an' riding in with that gal of Cain's, to boot."

"Well, call it whatcha like, but I just call it damn poor judgment."

"Yeah. You know, they say Cain beat the living hell outa two men for trying to see her after the cafe was closed."

"I hope that cowboy ain't too attached to his hide because the chances of him keeping it, least ways of all of it, are slim an' none. If the law don't git it, you can bet old Cain will. Yes sir, it'll be interesting ta see what comes of this."

Jesse ignored the stares and the whispers and looked at the town. There were several more buildings, but other than that, he could see no big change in it since he last saw it in '81. Mud town, that's how he thought of it. Not because of the muddy streets, since most of the time they were as dry as powder, but because of the adobe bricks that were used to construct nearly every building. Most structures were the same red color as the streets, with the exception of the few that had been whitewashed in front. Every now and then he saw one made out of lumber or rock, but if all the mud in Tascosa were to wash down the river, there would be very little left of the only town within a hundred lonesome miles in any direction.

Passing the business district, which totaled the metropolitan sum of two blocks, they turned north on McMasters Street and stopped at the most impressive-looking building in town—a two-story rock structure. Carved into a rock beside the narrow door were the words "ERECTED A.D. 1884."

Before Jesse could dismount, the door opened and a man appeared. He stood in the open doorway for a few seconds looking at the two riders, at the horses they were leading, and at the crowd of people gathering around. Then he looked at Tracey James and nodded his head in a gesture of recognition and greeting. Then he looked at the cowboy beside her, wrinkled his forehead and said, "Coldiron, what'n hell you done?"

Jesse grinned. "Howdy, Jim. I heard you'd quit punching cows an' got yourself a lawmaning job."

"Yeah," said the sheriff, still frowning, "and sometimes I don't know which is the worst."

The sheriff stepped out of the building and stopped in front of Jug. "Who's that?" he asked, lifting a thumb to indicate the two bodies behind Jesse.

"One's her brother," Jesse answered, looking at Tracey James. "I don't know who the other'n is."

The sheriff was a tall man, bare-headed, round-faced and wearing a dark mustache. He rubbed his chin for a few seconds and then said, "I reckon I might figure they got caught out in the blizzard and froze to death."

"Just figuring something don't necessarily make it so," Jesse warned.

The sheriff's eyes narrowed to a pinpoint. "How'd they die, Jesse?"

"Bullets."

"Dammit to hell!" The sheriff looked past Jesse. "Couple of you men grab ahold each one of them bodies an' carry 'em across the street to that empty shack. Jesse, you two better wait in my office while I go take a look."

While waiting in the office, Jesse thought about the man in charge of it. He had always considered Jim East a good man, a good cowboy. When he learned that East had been elected sheriff of Oldham County it had been a surprise. He always figured that the big ranchers would keep one of their own in office. If Jim East was a chore-boy for anyone, he had changed in the three years since Jesse had punched cows with him.

They sat in the sheriff's office for half an hour before Jim East came in the door. During that half hour they had been as mute as they had during most of the long ride from the line camp to town. Tracey spent the time looking out the window toward the south where cottonwood shadows lengthened along Main Street. Jesse rolled cigarettes and thought about his cattle.

When the sheriff returned he was all business. "The other man was Bill Lancaster, an outa work cowboy that hung around Hogtown." He circled the big scarred desk and sat down in the swivel chair behind it.

"Now, suppose you two tell me how this thing happened."

The telling did not take more than three-quarters of an hour, for neither knew much to tell. Tracey James spoke first and did so in a quiet, sad voice that grew even more quiet and sad when she described in detail the particulars that were painful for her. At times she dabbed at tears with trembling fingers, but never did she cry aloud, stop her story, or change inflection in her voice.

Jesse told his side in a straightforward, confident manner. Had the county sheriff been anyone other than Jim East, Jesse would not have told of his handiwork with the wire-pliers or his temptation to ride off for the rest of his cattle after finding the dead ones along the fence. He finished with, "I guess it's pretty plain that that Bill Lancaster feller is the one that Ward had trouble with before he saw me. Looks like they wound up by shooting each other, don't it?"

When Jesse was finished Jim East said, "Tracey, you'd better go on home and get some rest. The bodies are in the back of Farnsworth's store. They're fixing the coffins there, too. I'll be over in the morning and help you see that Ward gets a proper burial."

After she left and the door was closed, Jesse pulled the makings out of his pocket and rolled a smoke. He dragged a match across a leather boot sole, lit the cigarette, and stood. "Guess I can afford one night's room rent at the Exchange Hotel," he said as he put on his hat.

"Tell you what," Jim East said, "I'll save you the price of that room and put you up for the night at county expense."

Jesse removed the cigarette from his mouth. "What

49

the hell does that mean?" he asked in no polite tone. "Are you arresting me, Jim?"

"I'd rather just say that I'm putting you up for the night."

"Well I'll be! Is this the thanks Oldham County gives a feller for doing what's right? Jim, you know damn good and well I'm telling the truth."

The sheriff leaned over the desk and looked the cowboy in the eye. After a second he said: "Right now my hands are tied, Jesse. I'm sorry but I've got no choice, not for tonight anyway. I don't think you know what you walked into here. Hell, a range war's been trying to bust out here for over a year now. Nearly everybody in the county's on one side or the other. And you bring in two dead men—one from each side!"

"If you mean you're locking me up for my own good," Jesse said, "forget it. The first thing tomorrow, before daylight, I'll ride outa here and as soon as I find my heifers I'll be plumb outa the state. If there's one thing I ain't looking for, Jim, it's trouble. You know me better'n that."

"Like I said, Jesse, my hands are sorta tied on this deal. I'm locking you up tonight, but I'll be around early in the morning to let you go."

The jail was made of rock and set apart from the new courthouse, isolated among cottonwood trees on the east side of town. It consisted of a single small cell, ten feet by twelve, and did not match the courthouse in being newly constructed. There were steel bars on the two windows but the door was made of wood and secured from the outside by a hasp and strong lock reinforced by an ever-present guard.

As Jesse had feared, Jim East did not come around

early the next morning and let him out. Jesse paced back and forth in the small cell, whittled wooden matches into toothpicks and the toothpicks into tiny splinters, whetted his knife on the instep of a boot, and smoked one Bull Durham cigarette after another. Twice that day East did come by, but his visits were short and conducted through the locked door. They went something like this: "Hey, Jesse, can I get anything for you?" To which the voice from inside would reply, "Go to hell, Jim."

The only other person Jesse had contact with was Tracey James. Hers were business calls, not social. Jesse was surprised that first morning when the guard unlocked the door and there she stood wearing a long calico dress with her hair fastened up on her head, looking beautiful, but aloof and cold. When he spied the plate of food in her hands she answered his unvoiced question in a businesslike manner: "This is part of my job. The North Star is under contract to the county to feed the prisoners for a dollar a day and delivery. I've been doing this for two years whenever there is anyone in here." From then on, the mealtime ritual never varied from a formal "Thank you" from Jesse and a polite, cold nod from Tracey James. Brown eyes and black were careful never to meet.

Other than whittle, sharpen, pace, and eat, all the disgusted cowboy did was think. And, of course, he thought of his cattle, the main focus—the only focus —of his life. There were times, though, usually after she had picked up an empty plate and left a filled one, that he thought of Tracey James. Every now and then, he would picture the faint smile that he had caught on her face just before they had ridden into town. Before then, and ever since, she seemed incapable of any demeanor other than a solemn one. She seemed not only alone, but if he was any judge of women, which he was not, very lonely.

If these thoughts of Tracey James felt strange to Jesse it was because he was not used to thinking about a woman like her in any respect. The women he was used to having in his mind were the other kind, the kind who would go to the End of the World with a man and not think twice about doing it—the weather-beaten End of the World Hotel in Miles City, Montana, that is—as long as the man she was going with had enough silver in his pockets to defray her travel expenses upstairs and back.

But Tracey was no longer of any consequence to him, nor he to her. He had fulfilled his obligation to her when they arrived in town, an obligation, he now felt, he would have been better off leaving unfulfilled. If she wanted to be alone and lonely, that was her business. They had already agreed on that point. One thing for sure, just as sure as he looked forward to seeing her slim form in the doorway holding a plate of food in spite of himself, he had his own business to tend to. And just as soon as Jim East left that door cracked long enough for him to get outside, he would be two miles upriver before Jug's hoof dust settled on Main Street.

CHAPTER

6

How many countless millions of times it had happened before no man could say. But none in the Texas Panhandle had witnessed the event with less enthusiasm or more consternation than did Jesse Coldiron from the confines of the Oldham County jail. The routine never varied: The sun would rise opposite where it had disappeared the evening before, struggle to gain its zenith, only to abandon it at once and begin falling to the earth again.

Jesse had seen the cycle in its entirety twice from inside rock walls and through a barred window and was well into three-quarters of the third when the jailhouse door opened on its hand-forged hinges with a dry groan. In stepped Jim East, followed by a tall, angular man. It was obvious that they had not come bearing Oldham County's apologies.

"Jesse, let's talk," said East.

The prisoner was seated on the edge of his bunk. Without bothering to rise for his guests, he said: "Well, I'll be . . . I've been in this spider trap for three days while my cattle are scattering to hell'n back. For three days I've begged for somebody to talk to me, but no one would. Now I don't want to talk. All I want, Jim, is for you to get the shine of that badge outa your eyes long enough to see what's right and do it."

The visitors paid no mind to the "welcome" and made themselves at home. East sat on the bunk beside Jesse while the tall stranger hunkered down on his heels on the opposite side of the cell and said in a quiet voice, "Letting you out of here is what we come to talk about."

Jesse studied the stranger. He was no cowboy. Two things convinced him of that fact: the plaid wool coat over matching britches, and the long-barreled Colt strapped to his waist.

Jim East spoke again. "Jesse, this here is Pat Garrett." Then he paused to allow the name time to soak in—which it did. Like everyone else in the West, Jesse knew the name.

"Well, I'm not exactly Billy the Kid," Jesse said with his eyes on the long-barreled Colt.

Ignoring Jesse's remark, the sheriff said, "Pat's been sent here by the governor."

Jesse grinned enough to show a small chip on a front tooth. "And my paw said I'd never mount to much by being a cowboy. I bet he'd be proud to know that his boy had Pat Garrett *and* the governor of Texas wanting him."

Then it was Jim East's turn to grin. "Sorry to disappoint you, Jesse, but that ain't exactly the way it is. You see, Pat here was sent to put a stop to the cattle stealing going on in these parts. He's got some men working for him but they're having a rough time of it. This is still nearly all open range with cattle able to go where they pretty please, and there's a jillion square miles out there to prowl through. It's sure not much trouble for a man with some stolen cattle to disappear.

"I told Pat about you. I told him that you were a good man that had got himself in a little jam. He says he thinks he can help you but . . . Well, Pat, why don't you tell Jesse what you were telling me."

Coldiron sat on his bunk and looked down at the dirt floor. He could tell, just as sure as the sun was getting ready to slip beneath the rugged hills to the southwest, that he was not going to like this little set-to.

Pat Garrett unlimbered his six-five frame, stepped toward the bunk, and stuck out a long, thin hand. After ten seconds, Jesse stood and grasped the hand, shook it firmly, and then sat back on the bunk. Garrett squatted down on the floor in front of the other two.

"I'll get to the point, Coldiron," Garrett said. He pulled at the flowing mustache under his long nose. "I can see how your scrape happened, and I'll do what I can to help you. I've already told Jim that I thought we could drop the charges against you right now for lack of evidence. And on top of that, I'll do what I can to help you get your cattle back."

"I don't know how you dreamed up any charges to be dropped," said the cowboy, straightening his back. "And I don't figure on needing any help to get my cattle back."

The leggy lawman pursed his lips, stretched the mustache into a grin and said: "I don't think this is as simple a deal as you seem to, Coldiron. Oh, there may not be much that a grand jury would find to indict you on, but then we'd sure be within our rights to hold you here until a jury has a chance to decide. And I'll tell you something else, you can't ever tell what a jury might do. Sometimes they vote the way they want, in spite of evidence to the contrary.''

With those words the lawman paused, took out his pocketknife and whittled on a match. Finally, he looked up and struck out again. ''That new courthouse over yonder is brand spanking new. It's so damn new that this up-coming grand jury will be the first ever held in it. Now there's a story going around that you might be interested in: it has to do with LS Ranch loaning the county twenty-five thousand dollars to build it. That's not all, either. Apparently, the LS gave every one of their hands, I guess a hundred or better, a town lot here in Tascosa.

''Now, if you don't savvy what that means, I'll lay it out for you. It means those men will be freeholders in the County of Oldham, State of Texas, and will be eligible to serve on the grand jury. What I'm saying, Jesse, is that jury just might be weighted against you before it ever hears any evidence. After all, Ward James was an LS hand, you know.''

Garrett stood and dropped the knife into his britches pocket, stretched his back, and then roamed around the little cell. Jesse and Jim East sat on the bunk and said nothing.

Jesse was figuring. There was a good chance that Garrett was running a bluff about the grand jury affair. But if he was bluffing, it didn't show in his steel blue eyes.

Jesse was convinced that Garrett had said all that was on his mind. There had to be more to what was going on than he had been told so far, but he wasn't about to give Garrett the satisfaction of hearing him ask what it was. He would sit there until morning looking at the floor and the walls before he would ask.

The silence went on and on. Garrett settled down on the floor across the room from Jesse. East leaned against a rock wall. The room grew darker, and still no one broke the silence.

Coldiron pulled out the makings, rolled a cigarette, lit it, and smoked in silence until the butt was short enough to burn his mustache. He dropped it between his boots and crushed it.

Finally, Garrett slapped his hands on his britches legs in disgust and said, "Hell, Coldiron, we barely made a dent in the rustlers out there. It must have crossed your mind that whoever cut that fence and saved your cattle might not have had your best interest in mind. Hell, I'll bet you six bits that your cattle are in the hands of rustlers right now.

"The way it looks to me, if you sit here six more days waiting for that grand jury to meet, the chances of finding them are about as slim as a blade of winter grass. No, I think a man in your place would do anything . . ."

He was interrupted by the opening of the door. In it stood Tracey James. "Excuse me, it's supper time," she said. She raised the tin plate heaped with food to let them see it and walked into the jail.

Jesse got to his feet and stepped to take the plate. As he reached for it his right hand accidently encircled her left one. For an instant their eyes met, froze, and then just as quickly they both looked down, toward the plate. Jesse withdrew his hand from hers and took the plate in the other.

"Thank you," he said as the woman disappeared out the open door.

Garrett watched the cowboy attack the food. When

he could stand it no longer he said, "Dammit! Do you want out of here or not?"

Coldiron wiped his mouth with the back of a rough hand. "Garrett, you been chewing on something ever since you came in here. Why don't you spit it out before it starts chewing on you."

The cold eyes of the man narrowed. "Coldiron, we're ready to let you out of here right now. Just one thing—you help us, we help you. Can't get much simpler than that."

"Maybe we're getting somewhere now," Jesse said as he sopped a biscuit in cream gravy. He held the biscuit over his plate and said, "I think you know the song better'n I do, Mr. Garrett. So you dance and I'll eat."

At long last the hide was spread out where the brand could be read and it read something like this: Garrett needed a man to help him. A stranger who could get on the inside of the cattle thieves and supply him with information on who was stealing cattle from whom and how they were doing it. Jesse was a "goddamn natural." He had killed—it looked like he had killed, Jesse reminded him—a man who worked for the LS. And the LS was one of the main targets of the rustlers.

"I thought you said you already had some men," Jesse said.

"Oh, yeah. And they can catch the hell out of rustlers, too. But that's only in the saloons after a few drinks. Out there where the stealing's happening, they're useless as tits on a boar hog. And I gotta pay sixty a month to even get men like them. How would eighty a month sound to you, Jesse?"

Garrett wasn't through. He was saving the very best for last. He tried to make it sound as good as winning a tablestakes poker hand. "And while you're making more money than any cowpuncher ever has, you can be looking for your cattle. Now how can you turn down a deal like that?"

Silence returned to the enclosure. Jesse put his plate on the bunk and strolled across the floor to the open door. Out there, the long shadows had become no shadows. There was only enough lingering daylight to give individual identities to the leafless cottonwoods and willows.

"No deal," Jesse said without taking his eyes off the outdoors.

The lawmen exchanged glances. Garrett started to say something but the slim man at the door cut him off. He spoke in low, even tones, still looking outside. "I left home when I was fourteen years old. Never been back. . . . I guess the folks are long dead by now. I cowboyed on more outfits than I can count. By God, it was good, too. Lots of fun, wild living, and better friends than any man's got a right to expect.

"But one day I noticed something had changed . . . me, the times, I don't know, something. All of a sudden I realized that I hadn't been as free all those years as I thought. Do you know why? Because I was obligated to another man. As long as I worked for another man, then that man owned me, at least he owned my time. I started saving every dime I could so some day I could say that I worked for Jesse Coldiron. I wanted to know that when I got up in the mornings that it was Jesse Coldiron I was going to freeze or blister my butt off for and not somebody back east or across the ocean that didn't even know my name."

Jesse paused and drew a deep breath. After several seconds he went on. "Well, I had that dream, and I worked and saved and planned and worked and saved some more. Then last spring I quit my job, borrowed some more money and bought the heifers that caused me to wind up here.

"I still ain't worth nothing, more'n likely never will be, but it's me that I'm working for and it's me that I have to answer to. You're damned right. I *could* use that eighty a month. But then I'd be obligated to you and I don't want that. Not when I was just getting used to not being owned.

"As for my cattle? As long as they're alive and I'm alive, I figure I'll get 'em back. If they're not alive, then I'll go back to working and saving again. If *I'm* not alive, then it won't matter one way or the other."

Jesse turned toward the two lawmen. "The LS may own half the world. They may have built the courthouse and handed it to the county on a silver platter. And for all I know, they may own every jury that will ever sit in it. But I'll tell you one goddam thing they don't own—me. Now, you fellers either try the hell outa me or turn me loose, but I'm not for sale."

Less blunt language has dampened many a conversation. It suffocated this one completely.

As Jim East stepped past Jesse and through the doorway his eyes showed little emotion—Pat Garrett's showed less. Jesse watched as the twilight engulfed them. Before they completely disappeared from his vision the door was shut and locked and darkness flooded the jail.

The next morning gave every indication that Jesse's fourth day of imprisonment would be the same as the three preceding days. Tracey brought breakfast in a tin plate and coffee in a tin cup. Jesse offered a stiff, "Thank you," to the silent, stone-faced woman. Both were careful that the contact that had occurred the evening before, both of hands and of eyes, did not happen again. At noon the scene was replayed in an exact manner, except that beef and beans had replaced the bacon and eggs.

It was some three hours after Tracey had brought the noon plate that the door opened to the bright outside world. It was Sheriff East again. He said, "Follow me to the courthouse to get your things, Jesse. You're free to go. I'm sorry everything happened the way it did, but like I said, my hands were tied until Garrett had a try at you."

Jesse wasted no time in getting to the door.

"He give up already?"

"Nope. It seems like you had a witness to the shooting."

Jesse squinted his eyes. "A witness?"

"That's what he said, and he tells about the same story as you did."

"Who is it?" asked Jesse skeptically.

East flashed a sly grin. "Just think of the on'riest old codger you can."

"Well, that would be old Harlan Harrell but he's in . . ."

"Not anymore, he ain't."

"You mean . . . ?"

"That's right. He came in here about noon to get supplies and some of that rotgut whiskey he swears by. He said he saw the whole danged thing, and he knew where and when it happened."

As they crossed the vacant, sunlit lots between the old jail and the new courthouse Jesse was as happy as he had been the day he was able to swing the deal and purchase his heifers.

"Where is Harlan?" he asked when they entered the fresh-painted halls of justice.

"Left town. Said you could find him in Minneosa Canyon, if you were interested."

Having secured Coldiron's firearms from the courthouse, East led him a block south to Main Street and Mickey McCormick's Livery Stable. In there was everything else the cowboy owned in the world, besides his lost heifers: two horses, a saddle, and a light load of supplies carried by a little dun.

The sheriff waited until Jesse was in the saddle before he offered some farewell advice: "Go home. Let Garrett and his Rangers find your cattle. If rustlers have 'em, all you'll do is get yourself killed, or wind up back in jail—and I don't have time to keep getting your butt out of a sling. Go back to Colorado, and I'll get in touch when we find out something. You're getting a break, Jesse; don't be a damn idiot and start more trouble."

Jesse grinned big enough to expose the chipped tooth again. "Thanks for the advice, Jim. Sorry I can't take it. But I'm not going to be looking for anything but my heifers. Them an' that old cuss, Harlan." He lifted a hand in farewell, straightened in the saddle, and rode away from the livery.

CHAPTER
7

With every inch of his disgusted fiber, Jesse had fully intended to keep the self-made promise about being two miles upriver while his dust still hung above Tascosa's Main Street. Two things, however, prevented him from making such a swift departure. One was a balky dun packhorse that was not in much of a hurry to leave the accommodations offered by Oldham County. The dun's idea of a speedy checkout was no more than a sluggish, loose-jointed trot, and that in spite of the threat coming from the other end of his leadrope to "nail skids on those lollygagging feet with twenty-penny nails through the frog."

They had covered a scant half-block when Jesse was interrupted from his under-the-breath chastising of the little dun by his eyes falling on the other thing that delayed his leaving town—the North Star Cafe.

Jesse pulled up in the middle of Main Street and looked toward the whitewashed, adobe front of the cafe. Behind those mud bricks and curtained windows was Tracey James. The two of them had played leading—even though unwilling—roles in each other's lives for the past ten days. Their paths had become entangled as neither could have imagined. To not offer a final goodbye would be like leaving the last nail out of a hoof when shoeing a horse—it might not make much difference except for the nagging thought of something left unfinished.

Wheeling the horses to a hitching rail, Jesse dismounted and tied up. As he stepped onto the wooden veranda that fronted the cafe, the sound of shattering glass came from inside. Jesse reached for the door handle only to have it suddenly disappear, jerked to the inside by a man leaving in a huff. A big man. Square, heavy head like that of a herd-bull, hard blue eyes, red face, long scar on his left cheek. The man was wearing a string tie and a three-piece suit.

Jesse stepped aside to let the man stomp out, but instead of leaving, the man stopped and looked at the smaller cowboy on the porch. After measuring Jesse a moment, he pulled his hat down, shot a mocking smile toward him, and then sauntered out the door.

After watching the man walk off the porch, Jesse entered the cafe and removed his dirty hat. Tracey James was alone in the cafe, squatting beside a long table and picking up pieces of broken glass.

"Hello," he said. "Trouble?"

"Nothing I can't handle," Tracey said without looking up, her voice tart.

Jesse gave a nod toward the door. "Who was that nice feller?"

"Just a man," Tracey replied, more civilly. "Just . . . a man."

Kneeling beside her, Jesse helped with the glass splinters, putting his pieces into her outstretched apron. With the last piece off the floor he said, "I was just leaving town and I thought I'd . . . Well, I thought I'd say goodbye.''

"Mr. Coldiron," she said with a return of the sharp tongue, "for some reason, I believe what you said about the shooting, and I'm glad they let you out of jail.''

"Yes, ma'am," Jesse affirmed with a grin, "we can sure 'nough agree on that.''

"But not for the same reasons," Tracey said with a cold eye on the cowboy. "I'm only glad they let you out because I want the man that shot Ward first to be in that jail. For now . . . I don't think that man was you. Now, if you'll excuse me, I have things that must get done. Goodbye, Mr. Coldiron.''

Jesse said nothing else. He replaced his hat, nodded again, and went out to his horses.

When the door shut, Tracey moved closer to the window. As she watched the cowboy walk off the porch, untie his horses, and swing a leg over the big brown's back, she realized she had been short, maybe even bitter sounding. She had been that way without really meaning to be. It was part of the defenses she had built up over the years for self-protection: act cold, indifferent, sharp, and uncaring, never take a chance on giving a man the wrong impression.

Those were the rules she had lived by for years and they had served her well. She had thought she was respected by most of the people in Tascosa, and that was what she wanted more than anything in the world—other than for Nina and Ward to be healthy and happy. She had watched every move, every word. She thought she had gained respectability . . . until *he* found her again. But even then she would not let herself enjoy any man's company—even innocent conversation.

The truth was, she distrusted all men. She had made up her mind long ago to never let another man touch her, even though at times her young body yearned to be touched, to be loved. But she had smothered the fires of passion so well they were not rekindled for over a year.

Until the past few days.

Deep inside, she knew that was why she had been even shorter with Jesse than with most men. She felt something stir inside her that she did not trust. She felt it when their eyes met or they accidentally touched. She was ashamed to think that she had felt a tinge of it even before he had given up his chance to ride away and not come back.

Tracey's dark eyes stayed on him until he was past the end of Main Street. She would never see him again, which was for the best. But she wished for a moment that she had stopped him before he rode away and told him that she had not meant to be so rude.

Then she had a warming thought. A thought that brought a fleeting smile to her lips and an old ache to her heart: If he never came back, he might not ever hear the gossip; he might forever think of her as a respectable woman—cold, but respectable nonetheless. In that case, there might only be one man in the world who would remember her as she really was in 1884. One man whose picture of her would not be mounted in the marred frame of her past.

It was good to be on horseback again. Nothing felt as good to Jesse as a stout horse moving under him, especially when he was rested and feeling fit. If the four days in the ten-by-twelve-foot cell had done nothing else, it had given him time to rest and heal.

He crossed Tascosa Creek and its thick growth of trees at an easy trot. The November afternoon had a fresh, keen edge to it. The aroma of damp, rotting leaves along the creek gave way to the pungent odor of sagebrush. A quarter-mile past the creek a hill caught Jesse's attention. It was a little larger than the others nearby and flattened on top, but what attracted Jesse's brown eyes to it was the few wooden crosses, barely visible, on its crest.

When Jesse topped the hill, fifteen graves silently greeted him. Riding to the freshest mound of earth, he leaned over and read the inscription on the wooden headstone:

WARD JAMES
My Beloved Brother
1866–1884

"Eighteen years old," Jesse said to no one. Maybe he should feel some remorse for the boy in the grave, but he had not willingly put him there, and in his mind he had not really killed him. It had been so hard to see when it happened, and things had happened so fast that he had trouble remembering it all. The only sorrow he felt over the affair was for the sister Ward left behind, alone and bitter.

When Jesse started to turn away, another marker drew his attention. That one—three gravesites over—was noticeable because the mount under it was so small. Moving to it he read:

NINA JAMES
1880–1883
My Darling Baby

Leaning over with his forearms on the saddle horn, Jesse studied the tiny grave and the dried flowers on it. He looked over the tops of the cottonwoods bordering the creek to the cluster of rock and adobe buildings that was Tascosa. In a moment he straightened and rode toward the west.

Jesse looked at the sun. With any luck at all, Harlan Harrell would have company for supper. The thought of that made the cowboy grin with the first true happiness he had known since just before the first snowflake fell in Colorado.

CHAPTER

8

Jesse remembered the Canadian River country well enough to know that Minneosa Canyon was close to thirty miles upriver from Tascosa as the crow flies. But the Canadian River does not go as the crow flies, by a long shot. So Jesse decided to stay out of the twisting river bottom and cut across the sandy hills on the north. Unlike the south side of the river, the north side had few canyons that were big and rocky enough to hinder travel. He took in a lungful of crisp air, smelled the familiar odors of horse sweat and sagebrush, and put Jug into a jig of a trot and made him hold that pace.

The miles fell steadily behind. After a while, the cloudless western horizon shed all trace of the setting sun, and the evening star shared its blue-white brilliance with the rugged terrain below. Four hours after leaving Tascosa Jesse pulled rein on the rim of Minneosa.

Skirting the canyon's rimrock until he found a trail that led downward, Jesse gave Jug a slack rein and let him work his way to the creek bed below.

The creek bed was narrow and, like most others in the Panhandle, had known much more blow-sand than water. Hugh chunks of flint-hard rimrock had broken loose over the eons and had thundered their way down the steep sides of the canyon where they rolled into the deep sand of the creek to spend the next few eons. It was while Jesse was riding through these rocks that the night gave up its silence to so unique a voice that he knew in an instant who it was. Even though he had been expecting something of the kind, the suddenness and the closeness of that voice startled him.

"Now I don't reckon a man could draw bounty on man ears . . . but on jackass ears? Hell, who knows!" The voice was a blend of a laugh and a whisper and came from the closest rock behind him.

"Now, Mister-Comes-Sneaking-Through-the-Night, I wanna see that right hand of yorn full of bridle reins and helt up in front of the saddle horn, an' I wanna see that leftun in the air apalming them bright stars."

Three years had passed since Jesse had last heard that voice, and he missed it more than he had realized. It was a pure joy to hear it now, and all of a sudden he felt renewed and full of life. He felt like a kid again—and like a kid, could no longer contain his enthusiasm.

"Why you shriveled up old cuss," Jesse chided, "if you don't quit being so unneighborly I just might not help you get rid of that panther puke you call drinking whiskey."

"Coldiron? Is 'at you?" the voice asked, gay and gravelly. "Hee, hee. Well, I had a hunch it was, but a man can't be too careful around here. There's some bad hombres around here that's just as soon shoot a feller as to spit, and there's some others that are just as apt to shoot without meaning to. Everybody's as jittery as a turpentined cat and ashootin' at every racket they hear.

"Well, goddammit, you gonna just sit there all night like some stupid statue, or you gonna turn around so's I can see if you still got the looks of a leperosified horny toad?"

Jesse turned around and saw Harlan sitting on top of a big rock with his legs crossed. He was holding a long-barrelled Winchester and grinning like a leprechaun.

"I heard you was in Denver," Jesse said.

"Hell, I was for a spell. I figured I was too damned old to punch cows anymore so I went to my sister's to die. But, Jesse, there's so goddamn many folks in Denver a man ain't even got room to waller himself out a place big enough to die in. I felt as crowded as a sow bug under a stump, so I come back here to do my dying."

After a few more rounds of good-natured cussing the two set off down the creek. They rode south for a few minutes before Harlan turned his sorrel up a trail that led to a narrow meadow elevated to a slightly higher level than the creek but still within the protective walls of the canyon. Jesse followed him to a mound of earth.

"Hotel Harrell welcomes you," the old man said, holding his hat over his heart.

Jesse surveyed the place with one sweep of his eyes. He saw a dugout like hundreds of others he had seen across the plains. The only difference in this one was the rock front: most had to settle for one made of adobe bricks. A narrow slab door and a small window were built into this rock front and provided the only openings in the dugout. The roof was made by laying cottonwood logs close together and then covering them with a foot of Texas earth. A stovepipe six inches in diameter jutted up from the roof at an angle and gave off a thin cloud of gray smoke.

Built against the steep west wall of the canyon was a small horse corral made of barbed wire and crooked cedar posts. A spring bubbled up gently from under a pile of flat rocks on the uphill side of the corral.

Jesse and Harlan unsaddled, removed the pack from the dun, and laid saddles and equipment under a small lean-to. Jesse led the horses into the corral while Harlan threw their supper over the fence—two armfuls of dried mesquite beans. The horses arched their necks, squealed, and pawed the air a few times—as their kind does when meeting strangers—before attacking the mesquite beans.

"I trust," said Jesse as he chewed on a piece of beef, "that if I was to see the hide that this critter was wearing, it wouldn't have a Bar C on it anywhere."

"And I trust," Harlan countered, "that you or no one else will ever see this critter's hide. And I 'specially trust that you never will since you'd have to dig to do it, and I know how your hands fit a shovel handle, Coldiron." He grinned and wiped his mouth with the back of a hand and then went back eating.

And so it went. Supper was washed down with a steaming pot of black coffee as they covered the years that had passed since they last rode together. In the one-room hovel they hunched over a table made by placing a board over two empty nail kegs. The mesquite wood in the stove soon had the room at a cozy temperature. Two candles on the table cast giant dancing shadows on the walls. Yarns that had been told before were now shared again, and each man hung onto the other's words as if they had never heard the tales before. New stories were scattered among the old as something one said would remind the other of still another happening that was worth sharing.

They talked, as cowboys always do, of wrecks and storms they had been in or witness to; of horses and men they had known, both good and bad; of how good or how bad this or that outfit had been to work for; what this or that cowtown and the saloons and the women in it were like, and a hundred other things that good friends and cowboys can conjure up.

Coldiron and Harrell. They were famous in cowcamps and around chuck wagons far and wide for the shenanigans they pulled on each other and on other cowboys. It had been said that what the two of them had not done most likely could not be done—at least not by the type of men who wore out much more saddle leather than sole leather. They went their separate ways at times, but it seemed that somehow fate always brought them together again.

Even-tempered and good-humored, that was Harlan Harrell. Jesse had never known the old man to be mad. He always looked as if he was on the verge of breaking into a toothy grin, regardless of whether they were in the midst of a good time or a bad one. He had never said for certain how old he was, but Jesse knew he had to be pushing seventy summers, and pushing hard. The years of sun, wind, snow, and rain endured in the saddle had taken away from Harlan's physical abilities but had not diminished his love of life. He had never stood more than five-six, and now was shorter by a slightly stooped inch. If all of his pockets had been full of lead he might have tipped the scales at one hundred and forty pounds.

After the second pair of candles had been lit and

the stove stoked with more wood, Jesse said, "Well, are you gonna tell me about it, or am I gonna have to drag it out of you like pulling a calf?"

"I reckon you mean about my telling East I seen the shooting."

"What else would I mean? That's why I'm here to start with. If it hadn't been for that cockeyed story, I'd still be staring at the walls of that damned jail. Course, I'd still be having Tracey James fixing meals for me instead of the likes of you. But, if the truth's told, I guess I do owe you one, old timer."

"Yeah, you datgummed right you owe me, Coldiron. And you owe someone else, too."

"Like who?" asked Coldiron leaning toward Harlan.

"Well, if you'll just clam up a minute I'll tell you! Now that's better. You see, when I heard that Ward had been kilt I hustled to town to see about it and to see if I could be a hand to his sister—that's the Tracey you were slobbering over. See, I knowed both of 'em. Their old daddy and me went a long ways back. We started out punching cows together down around the gulf coast country. There weren't no big outfits then like there are now. Weren't hardly no cattle neither, 'cept the wilduns that nobody claimed. . . . Well, to make a long story short, Ralph—that was his name—married up and had a pair of fine younguns, Ward and Tracey. Then Mrs. James, she was a half-breed Kiowee *seen-yore-eeta,* and a mighty tailor-made one at that. She died, though, when the kids was barely off the tit. Don't remember what she died of—but old Ralph he never let them younguns dogie, not one little bit. He took care of 'em as good as anybody could. He brung 'em up here to the Panhandle in about '77. Ward was eleven and I guess Tracey was seventeen. God, Jesse, she was already prettier'n the law allowed then. They was getting on real good. Lived in Mobeetie and . . ."

Jesse knew the old man enjoyed talking more than anybody in the world. And when that old cuss got strung out and moving his tongue at a steady pace it took a hard bit and a tight curb to slow him down. Jesse could tell that there was no use straining himself any for the time being. He would let Harlan have his head for a while; let him run down on his own.

" . . . and right then was when Ralph ast me if'n I'd sorter keep an eye on the kids if anything ever happened to him. There was the worst kind of men in tarnation hung around those buffler camps. They was likely to cut a feller's throat just to see how far he'd run before he went to flopping like a chicken. And I'll be damned if it weren't but a little hitch after that, that someone bushwhacked Ralph and kilt him. So, when I heard about Ward I went to town to see about Tracey. She seemed to be holding up pretty good, considering. She's had more to handle in her young life than most folks have had to face in a long one. There don't seem to be no quit in her though. By God, that's some gal, Jesse. And just as sure as there's a coon in the corn crib, she's got looks enough to melt a man plumb down to the taler, too. Course, you being swore off women like you are I don't reckon you took notice of that, eh? Why . . ."

Jesse rubbed his tongue across the chipped front tooth and stretched his thin lips and wide mustache into a grin. "Well, yeah, I mighta noticed something of that sort once, but what I haven't noticed at all is you telling me how come you told East that you'd seen the shooting. In case you forgot, that's what you started out to tell me about an hour ago, but all I've been able to find out is about wild cattle and what the toughs in buffler camps do for fun.''

"Do you know what's the matter with you, Coldiron?'' Harlan said, his laughing eyes belying a smirk of disgust. "Well, I'll tell ya. You've never learned the finer art of explaining, and I have, and that's what's eating on ya. Hells bells, you don't just fly off the handle and get right into the grease without first you render the lard. You gotta lay groundwork, boy, and that's what I've been doing, and now that I got it done I'll get on with it. That is, if you can keep quiet long enough for me to get 'er said. Now, as I said, I went straight to the North Star Cafe in Tascosa and Tracey told me about you and the way you said the shooting happened. Well, she didn't say your name, just said a man. She told about you coming to the line camp all shot up and her fixing you up. She said you coulda just rode on when you got better but instead you took her back to Tascosa. She said she heard the deal the law put to you and that you must of turned 'em down because you were still locked up. She finally said that this feller punched cows here a few years back. That's when I ast what his name was and she told me it was you. I told her that I knew you, and that you'd stoop to most anything to keep away from honest labor, but that killing without cause was not one of 'em. . . . Then I went to see old Jim East.''

The bright-eyed old man had been enjoying himself up to now, but all of a sudden he grew more serious, the humor gone from his eyes. "Jesse,'' he said softly, leaning over the table, "that gal ain't never ast for nothing in her life, but I aim to do what I can to find out who sunk that first slug in Ward's belly. After their old daddy got kilt I didn't look after them kids like I promised I would. Oh hell, I went by Mobeetie now and then, but mostly I was so busy with myself I didn't see they needed help and were just too proud to ask.

"Take it from an old bastard that knows, Jesse, when you're young an' full of sap it's mighty easy to overlook them things that are real important. Any old fart, when he's seen as many summers as I have, can look back and see what he oughter have done, but it takes more than cow shit for brains and rye whiskey for blood to do 'em when they'll do some good."

The dugout became quiet. Jesse studied Harlan and was more than a little confused. He could tell the little puncher was wading ankle-deep in thoughts, seized by an unfamiliar melancholy attitude. Just as suddenly as this new and unexpected countenance descended on him it seemed to lift.

"So you finally got into the cow business, eh?" Harlan said as mirthfully as ever.

"I was in the cow business until a week ago," said Jesse. "Right now I don't think I could say that."

"How many cattle you short, Jesse?"

"The whole smear. I found twenty-five dead and the other seventy-three may be."

"Chances are they're still alive. Damn, Jesse, I never figured you'd stay with the notion of saving every dime for so long."

"It was you made me start thinking about it. Remember, when I was laid up with that broken foot, how you said that the times were changing so fast that before long you figured a cowboy would be just a rich man's servant?"

"Yeah," Harlan replied, "and I think it now more'n ever. God, how things has changed since me and you met up back in the sixties."

Jesse unlimbered his lanky frame from the crude chair, stepped to the stove and removed the enameled coffee pot. Taking only two steps he was back at the table and poured two tin cups full. Each time his foot hit the hard dirt floor his spurs jingled. He sat the empty coffee pot on the table, took out the makings, rolled a smoke, threw the tobacco to Harlan and said, "I guess things really went to hell around here after I left."

Harlan raised his eyebrows. "In a hand basket," he summed up. "And I can tell you about it damn quick—associations, rules, and cattle stealing.

"I can't tell you *why* people did what they did, all I can do is tell you *what* they did. The ranchers around here formed 'em the Panhandle Cattlemans' Association, and then they drawed up a set of the stupidest rules you ever heard of! Said no more branding of mavericks. Oh hell, they said it'd be all right to brand 'em as long as they were branded with the rancher's iron and not some old cowboy's. *That* they said was gonna stop. Said that since they built the drift fence there wouldn't be no more outside cattle, that *all* the cattle here belonged to some member of their goddamned association whether they was branded or not, and they better not show up wearing some cowpuncher's brand. On top of that, Jesse, they said cowboys couldn't keep any stock—cattle *or* horses—of their own."

Jesse twisted his head. "Godda . . . Not even horses?"

"That's right. Then a bunch of the punchers started up their own association, and its rules said they wouldn't work under those conditions for less than fifty a month, seventy-five for wagon bosses. About a hundred of 'em went on strike and was fired by the outfits. Some of 'em left the country like I woulda done, but the rest of 'em hung around to get even by stealing cattle. Now the ranchers have brought in Pat Garrett.

"I was here when the strike took place. I didn't sign no papers or strike, I just went to Denver to die. But it wasn't long 'til I was back here trapping critters. The outfits still pay me in a way. They pay me a five-dollar bounty on each varmint's scalp I turn in and the county pays another two. I got fifty-eight scalps last year an' they was worth over four hundred dollars. That's a helluva lot more'n I'd a made punching cows. Course, it ain't the same, I'd rather be cowboying on some good outfit. But I'm more my own boss now than I been in many a year."

"It's a heck of a note, Harlan," lamented Jesse, "but from what I've seen and heard there's a lot of places getting like it is here. It wasn't much better on that outfit in Montana but the pay was better. There's still some good outfits around, I guess, but they're getting as scarce as sugar ants in the outhouse. There's still places where there's grass, too, that nobody's claimed, but it won't last long—not like it looked like it would ten years ago.

"That's why I *got* to find my heifers, Harlan. I got to find a place and lay claim to it while there's still places to claim. There's no way a cowpuncher can save enough money to buy land and cattle too. I'm afraid if I have to spend another several years saving up enough to buy another little herd, I won't be able to find any grass. I figure this is my one and only shot at having anything more than a saddle and bedroll for the rest of my life."

The empty tomato can that had been pressed into service as an ashtray was half-full of Bull Durham cigarette butts, and the coffee pot contained but cold grounds. The mesquite in the stove had burned down to the point where only a few coals remained, and these were not sufficient to keep the chill of the high-plains night air out of the dugout.

The older man stood, stretched his back, walked to the lone cabinet in the room and produced a full bottle of whiskey. He smiled. "Always save the best for last. Let's take a couple of pulls on this and turn in."

He pulled the cork out of the neck and handed the bottle to Jesse. "I guess you will take a drink as long as someone else is buying, won't you?"

"On this night," Jesse grinned and said, "I'd take a drink even if I had to buy." With that he turned the bottle up and took a short drink, brought it down and made a face. "When I find them heifers and head 'em north, Harlan, I don't want to go alone. I want you to go with me. . . . Hell, we'll go someplace and start our own outfit an' if the management don't suit us we'll change shirts and have us a new set of bosses. We may starve a little and may go plumb bust, but we can give it a shot. It's not a hand I'm looking for, it's a partner."

Harlan took the bottle from Jesse's hand and swirled the whiskey around in it slowly. He lifted it toward his mouth. "Whatever's in the trail ahead of you, you don't need a mouthy old bastard like me tagging along."

"By God," Jesse came back sharply, "you're right, I don't need anybody to 'tag along.' And I'm not in the charity-offering business, either. If I didn't think you were as good a man as you ever were I wouldn't offer you the deal. After the heifers have all calved next spring I plan on heading west or north. I don't know where I'll go or what I'll find when I get there, but I'll need help and I don't have the money to pay anyone. You may not see any money for quite a spell. . . . Hell, maybe never. I ain't making any promises— that's why I offered you a partnership. We'll only sell what we have to, to survive, and put the rest back into the cattle. What do you say? You haven't lost your gambling blood have you? Hell, I've seen you bet a month's wages on which tit a calf would suck first.''

Harlan lifted the bottle to his lips and took a long drink. He looked Jesse in the eye, and after a while he spoke. "If I thought you was just feeling sorry for me I'd pro'bly whup your butt. . . . I'll think on it tonight. I ain't never been one to obligate myself, you know. . . . I'll study on it. Now let's water our lizards an' go to bed.''

As the dried-up husk of a man put the bottle away and went out the door to water his lizard, his blue eyes were drawing their own water. With his back toward Jesse he wiped at them quickly with the back of a thin hand.

CHAPTER 9

Beneath an overhanging rock high on a canyon rim a long-haired, spotted-bellied bobcat licked his paws, cleaning them of the blood from the night's hunt. Shortly, he would disappear into the rocks for the day. Life was good—his belly was full, the weather mild.

By the time the bobcat was satisfied with his cleanliness, a splash of crimson had been thrown over the canyon's eastern rim. He lay on his spotted belly without moving and looked down in idle curiosity at the two men coming from inside a hump of earth, saddling horses and riding in opposite directions: The man on the sorrel taking the trail that led to the eastern rim, the other finding a narrow deer trail that led between two boulders and finally topped out on the western rim.

Yes, Harlan would partner with his longtime compadre. He had no shackles holding him in Oldham County. But first, there would have to be two condi-

tions to the agreement. One was that the killer of
Ward James would be found and given justice; he
owed Ward and Tracey at least that much. Besides,
they could look for the killer, or the man he worked
for, at the same time they looked for the cattle. The
other dead man, that Bill Lancaster, had been riding
with some men who worked for a big, wheeling dealing cattleman who always seemed to have plenty of
cattle and money even though his ranch in the Panhandle wasn't big enough to keep a few head of
dough-bellied steers alive, if Jesse got his drift. Jesse
did.

The other condition to the partnership was contained in a greasy gunnysack that Harlan procured
from somewhere in the back of the dugout and threw
on the table as Jesse was finishing his breakfast.
Coyote and lobo wolf scalps. Fifty-seven by actual
count and worth $399 if the bounty was the same as
last year, and Harlan knew that it was. This would be
company money or old Harlan Harrell would go his
way and Jesse Coldiron could go his. He wasn't going
to sit in on the game and drag light—he'd have this
money on the table to win or lose, just like Jesse did.

The deal was sealed with a handshake, and in the
first seeing-light of day, the bobcat high up on the rim
witnessed the first official act of the Coldiron and
Harrell Cattle Company: to find the Coldiron and
Harrell Cattle Company cattle.

The plan the new partners drew up was simply to
separate and look for their cattle. Jesse could go west
and stay on the north side of the river until it made its
wide turn to the south. From there he would leave the
river and ride north until he reached the drift fence,
then turn back east, drift south, and wind up back at
the dugout the following evening.

In half an hour Jesse was peering down into Little Red Canyon, narrow and short and containing very little cattle-concealing brush. He was able to sit in the saddle, smoke a cigarette and search the entire canyon from its rim with his sharp eyes. There were a few cattle grazing in the early-morning frost, but they were straight-bred Longhorns and not the crossbreeds that he searched for.

Skirting around the head of Little Red, Jug trotted across a cattle-empty mesa and was pulled up at the rim of Red Canyon. All to be seen in it, from its yards-wide northern head to its half-mile-wide southern mouth, was thirty or forty wild turkeys scratching around in the dry, sandy wash that coursed its length.

Leaving Red Canyon, Jesse rode across another mesa. This one was bigger than the others, being a full mile across and ending above a tall, red escarpment that formed the east wall of Chavez Canyon.

Chavez was much more crooked and twisting in its configuration than either of the other canyons Jesse had seen that morning, and it contained something the others had not; something that always draws life to it like a candle draws moths. Water. A spring-fed stream. Not only did it draw all kinds of animals to the canyon, but it also caused a small forest of different kinds of trees and bushes to take up permanent residence there.

Chavez would require a ground-floor inspection.

After finding a trail and making the descent, Jesse saw many cattle. Most were straight-bred Longhorns with a scattering of Durham blood showing up in some of them. They were every color that a cow-critter could be, from duns to blacks to brindles to pure whites with black noses and eyes to reds. Some were solid colored and some were spotted and some were roan. Most were branded on both rib cages with a big LS. Now and then, he would see a cow or a yearling that wore some brand that either he did not recognize or that he could not read because of its haired-over condition. But no matter, he knew these could not be his for they were of the wrong breed, and none had had his seven-under-bit earmark cut out of their left ear.

Once he saw a big heifer standing alone beside the stream. She looked like she could have had the same breeding as his cattle. He was able to get close enough to see that she wore no LS, but he could never get to where he could see if she had his Bar C or not. Finally, she moved and looked straight at him.

Full-eared.

For a minute he thought he was back in the cattle business, but that untouched ear told him otherwise. The heifer must be a maverick, thought Jesse. He grinned. Another time, another place, a short hard run and a swift loop and she wouldn't be a maverick any longer. He was tempted to do it anyway. But if he were to be caught by the wrong people, old Harlan might become the sole owner of the Coldiron and Harrell Cattle Company on the same morning that he became a partner.

Leaving the heifer to go about her unclaimed way Jesse reined toward the mouth of the canyon once again and in a few minutes was emerging onto a large, sandy, sage-covered, river-bottomed flat. From where he was sitting in the midmorning sun, just outside the confines of the canyon walls, the distance to the river was but five hundred yards. But they were not five hundred empty yards. Instead, he could see several rock houses clustered on the flat. Chavez Plaza. Or was—now it was deserted and grown up with last summer's weeds and sunflowers. Tall brown grass was growing in the road that led into and out of the little village. Nature was reclaiming quickly what the Mexican sheepherders had worked so long and hard to build.

Suddenly the smell of death filled Jesse's nostrils. He rode toward the abandoned plaza, slowly, looking closely, following the stench. He circled three rock houses before the smell was overwhelming, coming from a big house on the southern edge of the plaza.

None of the houses had a door left on them. He stopped Jug outside the one where the smell was coming from, leaned over, looked into the dark interior. A pair of legs covered by homespun britches was dangling inches from the dirt floor in deathly silence. He had to dismount and stick his head inside the one-room house to see the rest of the sickening specter.

The man had been dead three, maybe four days. He was probably a Mexican, but the body was so black and swollen it was impossible to know for sure. Even though it was November and there had already been a killing blizzard, the warm weather since the storm had hatched blow flies and they were buzzing over the stinking corpse.

The man was hung from a cottonwood beam by a strand of barbed wire twisted around his neck. His hands were tied behind his back. A piece of paper was pinned to his front by a long mesquite thorn pushed into his belly. Jesse stepped through the door, quickly retrieved the note and hurried outside for fresh air. He found something else.

A little Mexican man was standing beside Jug, holding a cocked Winchester. "You gringo bastard," the little man said through clenched teeth, "eef you 'ave a god you must now make peace weeth him. You die now."

"Juan?" Jesse said urgently, hands raised. "Juan Castillio? It's me, Jesse Coldiron. I used to come by here a few years ago and eat watermelon with you. Remember?"

Jesse wondered how he ever recognized the man: his face was black and blue, his eyes swollen. Somebody had given Juan a good thrashing.

Juan held his rifle steady and said nothing. Jesse knew he'd best be talking while he was able. "I came here looking for some cattle, smelled something, and found him." Jesse nodded backward with his head, toward the house. "This was stuck on his belly." He held out the piece of paper he had never had a chance to read.

Juan held steady. "Read it."

Jesse brought the paper closer to his eyes and read: "This Mex bastard came looking for cattle. He got this instead. So will anyone else who comes around where they are not wanted."

Jesse lowered the paper. Juan lowered the rifle.

"You do not recognize my brother, Jesse?"

"You mean that's . . . Jose?"

An hour later Jesse and Juan had finished the grisly task of burying the putrefying body. When the last shovelful of soil had been smoothed over the grave they rested against a rock wall. Jesse rolled a smoke, crossed his chap-covered legs and said: "What the hell happened, Juan? Who killed Jose and gave you the licking? What happened to Chavez Plaza? I figured you folks would live here forever."

The truth is he hadn't thought they would live there forever. The handwriting had been scratched in the river sand by the time he headed north.

Juan's reply to that question was no surprise: "Just as zee grass she was coming this spring, Meester Lee, the L Yes Patron, he came in a fancy wagon and gave to our patron, Meester Chavez, some money and say it would be good if heem and all hees *empleados* they went back to Mehico. I do not know how much money it was, whether it was mucho or poco, but Meester Chavez he say that eef we stay we must likely fight the cow rancher. Heem say we no fight. By the time the plums they are blooming Meester Chavez and all his *empleados*, like my brother and me, we are in Anton Chico in New Mehico."

The Mexican grew silent again. Jesse scratched around in the sand with his pocketknife, looked at the fresh mound of earth, adjusted his hat, pointed his knife toward the grave and said, "What about the rest of it?"

Juan looked at the grave. "Ah, wheen we leave Chavez Plaza the five cows that belonged to Jose and me they were too beeg with calf to walk to Anton Chico so we leave them here. Many days ago Jose he came back to get them. When he no come back to Anton Chico I come to look at heem. Yesterday I meet three men up the reever between here and Salinas Plaza and ask eff they see our cattles or Jose. I tell them my brand and what my cows and Jose they look like. One of theesh men, a beeg one weeth a scar on hees face, he tell to me that my cows they are died and that Jose decided to move back to Chavez. Then the men they all laugh. I tell the man I look anyway, thank you. That eez when he told to hees *empleados* to hold me by the arms so he can teach to me that my cows they are died and that my brother made a beeg stink in Chavez Plaza and that eef I don't get the heel back to Mehico I make a beeg stink, too.''

"Juan," Jesse said, stuffing out a cigarette on his chaps and looking the Mexican in the eye, "I'm damn sorry about Jose. I came here to find my cows and I don't plan on leaving 'til I've got it done. If you want to ride with me, I'd be mighty pleased to have the company. We just may happen on to your cows, too.''

"No, Meester Jesse," Juan said, sad-eyed, "I go home now. Eef you had been the man weeth the scar I would have keeled you thees morning. But I go home now. I'm no scared of theesh men, Jesse, but my señora and my *niños* they need a life man more than they need five old cows.''

Juan stood and looked at the abandoned rock houses. "Ah," he sighed, "what a good time it was here, eh Jesse?''

When Jug lunged the last steep steps to top the rim above the Mexican ghost town, Jesse pulled him around for another look. Juan had told him that the other plazas up and down the Canadian were as forsaken and as lonely as Chavez. Borregos, Corsino, Jauquin, Ortega, Salinas, Trujillio. All of them abandoned, falling down. Bought out, run out, shot out, driven out, it didn't really matter, they were gone. It was another sign of the way things were changing and how fast they could change.

It didn't make him proud to admit it, but to be honest with himself he wasn't really sorry. Oh, he was sorry about the people, and especially about Juan and Jose; nobody should be treated like that. But the fact was, he had never been in love with sheep and thought any country was better off with cattle on it than a bunch of woolies. But dammit, somehow he knew he was in the same fix as the sheepmen: The best grasslands were being grabbed by the rich and the powerful. It was hard to impress on those kinds of people the importance of letting others run a few sheep—or a few heifers.

In the hour-after-hour ride since leaving the river he had seen many cattle; he had ridden to the top of many hills and sat there for long stretches of time and scoured the rolling prairie with keen eyes. Dark spots three miles away might be cattle. He would ride over and usually find them to be cattle all right, but they were never the particular cattle he hoped they would be.

Another hilltop. More dark spots in the distance. And another trot of a couple of miles that proved fruitless.

In this methodical manner he worked his way north until by the setting sun he was within sight of the drift fence again. He and Jug had been forty miles since leaving Harlan's dugout and had seen hundreds of cattle—but none of them his. This was a big, big country though, and seventy-three head of cattle could hide in it like a fly-speck on a crow's wing. Tomorrow he would work his way back toward the dugout and powwow with Harlan. If neither had found anything, they would split up again and search until one of them did.

Jesse was dead tired. He built a small fire from dried bear grass, chewed some tough beef jerky, and was in his blankets just after the sun had dropped beneath the hills to the west. He went to sleep listening to the hobbled Jug munching on dry grass and wondering if there could be any possible connection between the man with the scar he saw coming out of the North Star and the man with a scar that Juan Castillio had talked about. The last visions in his sleepy brain were opposites—the bloated body of Jose Castillio hanging by a piece of rusty barbed wire and the slim figure of a sad, dark-haired woman in Tascosa.

The first rendezvous after the formation of the partnership revealed that neither man had seen hide nor hair of a Bar C critter. They drew up new plans. Harlan would stay along the river and work back toward the east, keeping to the south side of the Canadian. Since no one knew of his recent entry into the cow business he could speak freely with anyone he happened to meet. Who knows, a word dropped here or there to an old trapper who didn't know anything but skinning knives and scalp lice might just be enough to let the stink out of any rotten egg that might be laying around.

Jesse would also work east in much the same manner as he had worked west two days ago. If he found nothing he could drift into town, over Harlan's verbose objections, and see if he could hear any talk around the saloons that might have to do with stray cattle.

"Say," Jesse said as they were making ready for bed, "there was a couple of things that happened after I got outa jail that I've been aiming to ask you about. The trouble is I haven't got you to stop talking long enough for me to speak. They're both about Tracey. . . ."

"Goodgodalmighty, ain't she some gal!" the old man wheezed. "Why, if I was just forty years younger I'd shore 'nough be . . ."

"She was having an argument with a man when I went in the cafe. A big good-looking man with a long scar on his cheek. Know anything about him?"

"Hell, yeah. That was J. W. Cain, the man I was talking about that's got a dough-belly ranch on Cheyenne Creek. They say he's got a bigun in New Mexico, but I don't know about that. What I do know is that he always has lots of money and the men with him look more like gunhands than cowboys. He's trouble, mister, and I mean with a big T. He likes to act like a big-shot rancher, but I say he's playing both side agin the middle. I mean, he's chummy as a puppy on the porch with the big outfits, but he's a sneaky bastard that's taking advantage of the outa-work punchers by having 'em do his dirty work."

"You still got my attention," Jesse said. "What dirty work?"

"The way I figure it, he's stealing cattle. Could be that he's got ourn, too. But they wouldn't be at his ranch, they'd be hid somewhere else. So, we just gotta keep prowling 'til we find 'em."

Jesse told about Juan and Jose Castillio and the story about a big man with a scar on his face being involved.

"Yep," said Harlan, "I'll bet you two bits that was the same lovable J. W. Cain. He's a real good hand when it comes to being a son of a bitch. You wanta steer clear of him, Jesse."

"Well, what the devil he's got to do with Tracey?" asked Jesse.

"Hanged if I can figure that one out. I'm shore she ain't got nothing to do with the likes of him. If I had a hunch, which I got, I'd say that he's been trying to snort in her pretty flank and she's been wheeling an' kicking the hell outa him." Harlan chuckled.

Harlan made his nightly trip to the whiskey cabinet and produced the dark tonic once again. After Jesse took his obligatory drink and handed the bottle back he said, "I was going to ask you something else. I stopped by the graveyard above town that same day and saw a little grave close to Ward's."

"Yeah?"

"Well, I was wondering whose grave it was. The headstone said Nina James."

"There's a good reason for that, that's what her name was."

"Whose name?"

"Well, I'll be. . . . That's what the little girl's name was that's buried in that grave. Sweetest little girl that ever drew breath: curly hair, bright eyes, big smile."

"But," said Jesse, "whose little girl was it?"

"Tracey's."

"Tracey's?" Jesse paused. "Where in the hell did she get a little girl?"

"Jimmy Christmas! Where in the ever-loving hell do you reckon she got it? Coldiron, sometimes I thank you shoulda gone to town a mite more regular with the boys. Where did she get a baby! Cry-moe-nee!

"I'll tell you where she sure-as-the-hubs-of-hell-are-hot didn't get it, Coldiron. There didn't no spindly-butted, pillow-feathered stork brang it. Now, I'll let you see if you can cipher the rest of it without no more help from your elders."

"Dammit, Harlan," Jesse said more serious, "tell me about that baby."

The slim form fairly whirled across the earthen floor, swung open the door and said over his shoulder as he stepped into the darkness: "Time to water my lizard and hit the sack."

CHAPTER
10

Tracey sat by the dry mound of red earth. It was time for her to get back to town; the supper customers would begin coming into the North Star soon.

She looked at Ward's grave. Last Sunday she had buried him. A week later the pile of dirt covering him was already sinking. Soon it would be no higher than that covering Nina. Ward and Nina. Both dead.

How could that be?

Things had seemed so good, so right, after they had made the move to Tascosa. How could they turn out so bad? Maybe it was her fault after all. Maybe it was part of her punishment for what she had done. No! She couldn't believe that God would take the lives of two people as innocent as Nina and Ward just to make her suffer.

But there the graves were. They were both dead. And she had suffered. Suffered ever since he found her again.

October 8, 1883. She remembered the exact day it happened; the day her world in Tascosa began to

crumble. Maybe there should be a tombstone between Ward's and Nina's graves with her name and
that date on it because since then she had not had
much of a life.

She could still feel the shock and the dread that
gripped her that beautiful fall day when he walked
into the cafe. He was wearing a fancy linen shirt with
ruffles on the front, a fancy black frock coat and a
bowler hat. Dressed like that he stuck out like a sore
thumb, and that was exactly what he wanted to do—
always, anywhere.

She was busy with other customers and didn't pay
him much mind as he took his place at the long dining
table. When she placed a bowl of food before him she
heard him say something to a man seated beside him.
His voice froze her. She grew tense with anxiety, like
a cotton-tailed rabbit hearing the wind rushing over a
hawk's wings. Where had she known that voice and
why did it repulse her so?

Then she looked at him and saw the scar. Then she
knew.

In her heart she had known that he would come,
sooner or later. Of course he would come. What had
happened between them would follow her for the rest
of her life. She had been a fool if she ever believed
otherwise.

Two years, a hundred frontier miles, a different
town, and he had found her.

That night he had come to her room behind the
North Star. She fought with her terror and let him in.
She had to face up to him and make him think that
she was not afraid.

When he stepped into the lantern light of the small
room she turned her back to him. Nina sensed the
fear in the room; she ran to her mother's side,

hugged her leg and tried to hide behind her long skirt.

"Hello there, little girl," he said, "I guess you don't remember me. Me and your mother used to be real close friends. Come here, I have some candy for you."

"No!" Tracey said and hugged Nina closer to her legs. "You never, never take anything from that man."

"Now Tracey, that's no way to warm up an old friendship," he said.

Tracey turned to face him. "We never had a friendship and you know it," she said coldly. "Why have you come here?" But she knew why he had come.

"You're right, Tracey," he said with a lecherous smile, "we had a hell of a lot more than a friendship, didn't we? But we had nothing compared to what we can have now."

"What happened in Mobeetie was a mistake, and I'll take most of the blame. But it was a one-time mistake that will never happen again." Her voice was firm and steady.

"Yeah," he said, "you made a mistake all right. But I'm the kind of man that can forgive. And just to show you how forgiving I am, I'm willing to keep our little . . . what shall we call it? An affair? Yes, I guess that's a good term for it. I'm willing to keep our little affair in Mobeetie," he fingered the red scar on his cheek, "a secret. I'm sure you'd rather not have the whole town of Tascosa know all the intimate details."

"Get out!" Tracey yelled.

"My, my, such a loud voice from such a pretty lady. You didn't let me finish though. As I was saying, I'm willing to keep our former affair a secret. Now that's because I'm kindhearted and forgiving. But I'm also a good businessman, as you know, and it's not good business to give something for nothing. All you have to do in return is to . . . We are having trouble choosing the right words tonight, aren't we? Let's just say that all you have to do is to be friendly—make that real friendly—with me.''

He looked at her and grinned. Then he pulled a cigar out of a vest pocket, bit off the end of it, and held it in his mouth with one hand while he held a match to it with the other. After he puffed on it enough to get it lit he smiled again and said, "I've got a lot more money now than I had in Mobeetie, Tracey. You be nice to me and I'll do a lot more for you than just keep our secret. I'll make you the envy of Oldham County. You'll never have to work in a greasy dump like this again. I've got a little ranch just west of here a couple of miles and a lot bigger one in New Mexico; you pick which one you want to live on. Or you and the girl can move into the Russell Hotel here and I'll pay all the bills. How much kinder and forgiving can a man be than that?''

Tracey gritted her teeth, narrowed her eyes. "I made a mistake in Mobeetie, all right, and that mistake was that I didn't cut you a little bit lower, just under the chin would have been about right. You will never have anything I want. Now get out of here and go tell everybody you see about my past. But I am not for sale.''

Cain quickly closed the six feet separating them and grabbed her by the hair. He bent her head back and she was powerless to move against his big frame. The mock smile was gone now from his face and in its place was a predatory snarl. He spoke with a deep voice through clenched teeth. "Now you listen to me, you little bitch, I mean to have what was rightfully mine back there in Mobeetie. You can give it easy and we'll both enjoy it, or you can give it hard and I'll enjoy it by myself. Makes no difference to me. Either way I aim to have you, and I aim to have you from now on. I'll give you time to think about it. While you're thinking, just remember that you're mine and I'm not a sharing kind of man. You go to brushing up against some cowboy and trying to get him to take you away from here, just remember that all you'll do is to get him killed.''

He then mashed his big face against hers in a violent kiss that caught her lip between his teeth and hers and brought blood to it. She pounded on his chest to no avail. Nina cried and screamed and he did not stop. Tracey feared he had changed his mind about giving her time to think about it. Suddenly, without planning, she opened her mouth and bit down with all her might on his lip. She tasted blood and knew it was not her own this time. He jerked loose and slapped her, blood trickling from his lips. Then he smiled and walked out the door.

A tense two weeks dragged by and she had heard no more of her past. Maybe, she hoped, it had crawled back to whatever dark, damp place things like that go to when they are not tormenting those who mistakenly gave them life in the first place. Maybe Cain had more feeling than she had given credit for.

No, she soon found out, she was wrong on both maybes. She could never pinpoint an exact day that people began treating her differently; it was a gradual change that required several days' accumulation to be discernible at all. Then one day in the cafe she realized that Cain had been talking. She had no way of knowing what Cain had spread around, although she suspected not the whole story. But even the truth would have ruined her in the eyes of most people.

She became aware of the reproachful stares of the

women on the streets, and most of the men looked at her in that same salacious manner that she had been forced to accept in Mobeetie. If Mr. Sheets ever heard the talk—and she was sure he had—he never said a word; he treated her in the same businesslike manner he always had. For that she would always be thankful. But she wondered how much longer it would be before he would be forced to let her go. She could tell the type of people coming into the cafe had changed some and that there was more of a ribald atmosphere there than she had known before Cain found her.

When he was not at his New Mexico ranch, Cain was the most faithful customer the North Star Cafe knew. He was obsessed with Tracey. Like a fanatical art collector who feels he must possess what others are content to admire from afar, so it was with J. W. Cain. There was nothing in Oldham County as apt to turn a head or raise an admiring eyebrow or cause wind-chapped lips to pucker in silent whistle than the face and figure of Tracey James; that which finished second—and to all but the very young or the very old, it was a distant second—was a well-made, good-headed cowhorse. Cain couldn't have cared less about the cowhorse—that was but a toy of the working class—he was after number one.

That fact alone would have been enough for him to decide that Tracey would be his, but when that was added to the fact that he had something for which his ego—not to mention his face—still demanded revenge, the sum came up to a six-foot-four hulk of a man who was as dangerous as a locoed bull buffalo when he noticed that any other man so much as talked to Tracey twice in the same week, other than strictly business in the North Star—and even that was suspect.

As for Cain's warning to Tracey to not "go rubbing

up against some cowboy," he could just as well have saved his breath. For the many months she lived in Tascosa before he saw her she was doubly careful to never give any hint whatsoever of any impropriety with the opposite sex. If she so much as smiled at a man it was but a cold, polite one as he paid for his food in the cafe. After Cain started stalking her she was even more cold, more distant. Even so, she heard rumors of him whipping men on at least two different occasions for being too friendly toward her.

One would think that fate would have had more to do than make still more trouble for a single, young mother struggling to make a life for herself and her daughter. But no. On a blustery night in late December, barely ten weeks after Cain had come to her room, Tracey was dealt the severest blow of all— Nina came down with the fever and died. One day she had been her normal, cheerful self, running and playing. Four nights later, as the searching wind banged shutters and doors up and down Main Street, she died, in spite of all the nursing, promising, and praying that her mother could do.

After watching Panhandle soil shoveled over her fair-haired, ashen-faced three-year-old, she found that Mr. Sheets was kinder to her than ever. He gave her time off just about anytime she requested. She could get a horse at the livery stable just down the street and ride alone in the canyons and hills of the open range nearby. Sometimes she would even ride out to visit Ward when she knew he would be alone in a line camp. On those longer rides she wore men's clothing, considering it safer to look like a man, at least from a distance, rather than a young woman alone. This habit didn't help her already-tarnished image one iota with some of the area's primmer citizens. Respectable ladies did not wear britches or straddle a horse like a man. None, that is, but Tracey, and her respectability was in her own heart and in the few people who were content to judge her on her life as they observed it, and not as the sordid stories going around town depicted it.

Many times she would ride no farther than the little flat-topped hill on the west side of town, or other times after having ridden beyond, she would stop by it on her way back to town. That particular hill, of course, was the one that contained the town graveyard, rocky and short on vegetation but quiet and peaceful nonetheless. On top of that hill she would sit and watch the world go by. Tascosa was just below, across the tree-lined creek, which wound its way to the north through taller hills before leveling out on the prairie. To the south a scant quarter-mile was the wide Canadian River, with the brush that hugged its water-soaked sandy banks; to the west—her favorite direction—were the many canyons, buttes, and mesas, looking soft and blue in the distance.

Here, alone, away from town, was a side of the slim beauty that most never saw. They saw only the stolid and determined and, some said, hardened Tracey James. But here the feminine and fragile Tracey would sit on the cool earth by her baby's final home, chin resting on her knees, watching the sun drop toward the twisting river.

Two weeks and one day after Jesse first entered the northwest corner of the Panhandle, thinking he would have his heifers home in no more than three days, he was riding along the road that would shortly deliver him to Tascosa; the town that he had ridden out of five days ago vowing to never return. He had seen no more sign of any Bar C cattle, and in spite of warnings to the contrary, he was going to town.

Jug trotted by the hilltop graveyard, and the sight of an empty-saddled horse interrupted Jesse's cattle thoughts.

When Jesse reached the top of the hill, Tracey had her back to him, arms around her legs, looking toward the gathering shadows of the broken country to the west. She wore a plaid dress like the one she was wearing that day in the cafe. This time, though, her hair was not bunned up on top of her head. Instead, it tumbled down her neck, over her shoulders and halfway down her back. Hair as black as a crow's shadow and as thick and soft-looking as a prime wolf pelt.

She sat beside her baby's grave, still as death itself. Jesse started to speak, hesitated, tried again, and again stopped. Now he turned and took a step toward his horse. He suddenly felt as though he had no more business up there than a remuda bronc did in a show ring.

Just as his left hand grabbed a fistful of mane and his raised foot toed up the stirrup to hoist his frame into the saddle, Jug took it upon himself to blow his nose. The rattle coming out of his nostrils cut the graveyard silence like reveille at daybreak.

Jumping to her feet and whirling about, Tracey held her hands close to her breast, and gasped and said, "Oh! You . . . scared me."

Caught now with no retreat possible, Jesse took his foot out of the stirrup. "Sorry, ma'am," he said, embarrassed. "It looked like you were . . . I mean . . . Well, I didn't mean to bother you none. I was headed to town and saw a horse up here by the graves. . . . But then I saw you by the little one's there and I thought, I'd better not . . ."

"It's time for me to be getting back to town anyway, Mr. Coldiron, so if you'll excuse me."

Jesse watched as she walked stiffly to her horse. She untied the reins from a low-growing shrub and pulled the cinches on the saddle tighter.

"Oh yeah," Jesse said before she could mount, "Harlan wanted you to know that he aims to find the man who shot Ward that first time."

"Thank you. Have you found your cattle yet, Mr. Coldiron?"

"Not yet. That's why I came to town; to see if I could find out anything from loose talk at the saloons."

"Yes," Tracey said, "I'm sure you'll hear a lot there." Then she turned to the horse and mounted.

"Ma'am . . . Tracey," Jesse said as he watched her turn the horse around, "I'm not much count at this sort of thing but I got something that needs to be said. I hope you won't mind."

Tracey stopped the horse and turned him back to face Jesse. She looked at him for an instant and then looked into the distance and waited.

"It seems that you've had a real run of hard luck. . . . I mean, even before I came along. And then I made things worse for you, even though I didn't plan on it. I'm sure enough sorry. Not just about Ward, but about the other things, too. Harlan told me some of it. If there was any way I could help. . . . But I don't guess there's much that I can do."

With her dark eyes still looking for something far away, Tracey said, "Is that all, Mr. Coldiron?"

Jesse looked at the ground a moment, then he looked at her. "Yeah . . . except that you're too young and pretty to waste your life away mourning things that can't be undone."

There was an awkward silence while Tracey looked into the distance and Jesse looked at her.

"Well," Jesse said turning to mount, "I reckon I'll wander on into town."

"Thank you, Mr. Coldiron," Tracey said without yet looking at him. "What did Harlan tell you?"

"Just told me about your little girl, and what a cute one she was."

Tracey turned her big eyes on the cowboy. "There's a lot he hasn't told you about me, Mr. Coldiron." Then she smiled.

It was the second time Jesse had seen her smile, but this one was a knowing kind of smile and nowhere near a happy one.

Jesse mounted and Tracey started her horse off the hill. She stopped halfway down and turned to look uphill. "If you haven't eaten," she said flatly, "you could come by the North Star later, Jesse."

It was the first time she had ever used Jesse's first name, and that fact was not lost on either of them. The point they were both mulling over, as Tracey's horse leveled out onto the clearing between the graveyard and the creek, was what it meant, if anything.

CHAPTER

11

Jesse did not take long to ponder the ambiguous invitation to drop by the North Star Cafe. He had business to attend to, but he rode the length of Main Street without stopping. He felt certain his business could best be conducted in Hogtown.

Hogtown was a part of Tascosa that had formed a half-mile east and a little to the south of the main town. Its earthy name came from the fact that in a municipal election the residents of Tascosa voted that this lower portion of town would be the only part where hogs could be kept within the city limits. This arrangement suited both divisions of the town and the squalid-sounding name that accompanied the election results would—as long as the town lived—replace the more mundane title of Lower Tascosa.

Besides the half-mile of sandy road and the porcine inhabitants, there was something else, something much more isolating and dividing that separated the two parts of town. Just about everyone in the county was on one side or the other as far as the undeclared war between the big ranches and the striking cowboys was concerned. It so happened that the element that was opposed to the big outfits wielding all the power in nearly every aspect of life in the county, from politics to employment, had its unofficial headquarters in Hogtown.

Here the striking cowboys had whiled away their idle time while waiting for the ill-conceived strike to take its toll on the members of the Panhandle Cattlemens' Association. Since the businesses in Hogtown were raking in good money from the cowboys, they catered to them and gave at least verbal support to their cause. When it was apparent that the strike had about as much chance of working as a sore-backed horse did of pulling a cow out of a bog, the ill will between the two parts of town had created an unfordable barrier, at least socially.

The businessmen in Upper Tascosa could not afford to give much support to the strikers even if they did happen to think that it would be good for the big operators to be brought down to ordinary-people size. The outfits that did business there covered as much land as some entire eastern states and spent more for supplies in a week than all the twenty-five-dollars-a-month cowboys would in several years.

So Hogtown belonged to the little man, the often out-of-work cowboy and those who supplied him with whatever little merchandise he might need and could afford to pay for—which was very little after the first few weeks of the strike. Here, the cowboy who had the audacity to challenge the big-money men found his whiskey, his food, an outlet for his gambling urges, and women who, for a price, catered to urges of a more personal nature. So there will be no mistake about it, the folks in Upper Tascosa also had the same needs and urges as those in Hogtown; and there were the same types of establishments there as could be found to the southeast. The only difference was a little more polish to the counter tops, another lantern or two on the walls, a little less water in the whiskey, and smaller waists and fewer years on the women.

Jesse entered a low-roofed adobe building called the Edwards Hotel and Saloon, angled across the warped plank floor and bellied up to a bar that extended across the entire north end of the saloon. Three men were playing cards on a table made from a shipping crate and four more were shooting dice on the floor next to the south wall. Jesse heard the dice tumble across the floor and bump against the wall. Every time they bumped a loud string of cussing and cheering by the respective losers and winners filled the interior of the dimly lit room. Two buxom, hard-faced saloon girls were standing over the four kneeling cowboys and making raunchy side bets with them at each roll of the ivories.

The man behind the bar was a big-bellied, broad-faced man with a full mustache. He seemed as oblivious to what was going on in the room around him as the soot-blackened globes on the two lanterns that hung on each wall.

"Whiskey," Jesse said.

The bartender poured a drink from a half-gallon bottle that was all but hidden by his huge hand.

Jesse tossed the drink into his mouth, felt it sear his throat and insides. While he was wondering if he should order another before the numbness left his throat, the card game broke up and the three men walked toward the bar, high-heeled boots and big-roweled spurs noisy on the drum-hollow floor.

"Ain't seen you in here, 'fore," the whale-bellied bartender said without looking up from the counter he was wiping.

Jesse wondered for a second who the man was talking to. "Nope," he said after he knew the man was talking to him. "I just got in town."

"Staying long?" The bartender still had not looked up.

"I reckon that depends," Jesse said, measuring each answer.

By now the three men who had been playing cards were leaning on the bar to Jesse's right. The bartender sat three shot glasses on the greasy bar and filled them with whiskey.

The man standing next to Coldiron, average size, clean shaven, bucktoothed, said, "You say you just got to town, cowboy?"

"Yeah," Jesse offered, disinterested.

"You looking for a cowpunching job?"

"Depends," Jesse said, looking at his empty shot glass.

"Well, by God," injected a tall, cadaverous-looking man who stood in the middle of the three, "there ain't none 'round here. Not 'less you wanna work for some goddamn outfit that'll treat ya worser'n some nigger."

The bucktoothed man next to Jesse flashed a wry grin and said, "I reckon now, Slim, that that sorter depends on what kinder cow gathering a man is up to."

The big bartender joined in, still with his eyes on the counter, "This here's the feller they had in the county boarding house, the one that brung in Bill and the James kid."

This revelation brought a silence to the tavern. The men at the bar said nothing. The crap shooters held their dice. Jesse had no idea how he stood with these men. Ward was a big-outfit hand so was probably not loved by them; but Bill Lancaster could have been one of their own.

In a moment the somber atmosphere was sliced by a congenial remark from the man called Slim. "That sonabitch had a killing coming," he said, hollow-eyed and vengeful.

Jesse studied Slim's words carefully and thought they smelled like a baited trap. "Which one?" he asked.

Without hesitation Slim shot back, "Hell! that James kid. It weren't no skin off his back if we cu . . ."

His words were cut off clean by a cold voice from the doorway, not loud but low and threatening, like a growl coming from a dark cave. "Goddammit, Slim, I know you boys got some supplies to load."

The man's six-four frame filled the doorway to capacity and left no room for the anger to escape. He stood high-dollar dressed and important, waiting for the men to carry out his implied orders. They did. He side-stepped to let them out into the afternoon, then walked to the bar.

The bartender tilted a bottle of whiskey in his hand and looked a silent question. The man nodded, threw the drink into his mouth and swallowed it. Only then did he turn to look at Jesse.

The heavy muscles in the man's jaws bulged, the red scar on his left cheek twitched, the eyes were pools of blue hatred.

"You must be Cain," Jesse said with as much feeling as a marble slab.

"I am," the man said, his voice sharp, "and if I was you, I'd be moving on. It looks like you might get off for killing that kid, but I wouldn't push my luck too far."

After a time, Jesse turned slightly toward Cain, looked at him, wondered what he could have to do with Tracey, thought of a stinking corpse in Chavez Plaza. "If that was advice, I reckon you can go to hell."

J. W. Cain puffed up. The scar on his cheek darkened. He wheeled about and stomped toward the door. Before he reached it he stopped and turned.

"Just one more piece of *advice*. A man that prowls all over a country where he hasn't got any business can only blame himself if he comes up missing. Especially, a country as worked-up as this one is. I wouldn't think a handful of cows would be worth getting killed over. Besides that, I was at the county commissioners' meeting today at the courthouse, and as of now you don't have any cattle . . . if you ever did."

After leaving Hogtown Jesse rode back to Upper Tascosa and went straight to see Jim East at the new courthouse. There he learned two events had occurred that day in the courthouse and at least one of them had a direct influence on the corporate health of Coldiron and Harrell. East gave him the news like a double shot of rye whiskey: "Jesse, the county has outlawed your brand and laid legal claim to any cattle wearing it."

"Hell! they can't . . ."

"They've already done it, Jesse. Don't take it personal though. Since September nearly any brand that's not owned by one of the big outfits has been outlawed by the commissioners. And a man would be hard put to hold it against them, too. Some of these cowboys around here went haywire when that strike didn't work. They're not just branding a few mavericks, Jesse, they're out-and-out stealing. On top of that, some outside rustlers have moved in and have been giving the ranchers pure hell. It might not be the best way to handle it, but politics will be politics. If I haven't learned anything else since I pinned on this badge, it's that.

"The Cattlemens' Association felt that the only way to get a handle on the stealing was to outlaw nearly any brand that's not an established one. And since one of the commissioners is J. E. McAllister, the manager of the LS Ranch, and the county judge owns the biggest supply house in the county and depends on the big outfits for business, it was only natural that the commissioners agreed with the Cattlemens' Association."

"What'll happen *if* they find my cattle?" asked Jesse.

"If they find 'em they'll sell 'em, and the money will go to the county, and there won't be anything you can do about it."

Both men grew silent for a few moments until suddenly Jesse said, "Has the county found any of my cattle?"

"No," East assured him.

"Then how come they outlawed my brand?"

"A man was at the meeting this morning and he told the commissioners that he came upon a man branding a maverick last week. The man got away but left the maverick tied down, and it was a Bar C that had been branded on it."

Jesse stood slowly. "I'll bet a dollar to a thin latigo that that man's name was J. W. Cain."

"It was," East affirmed, "and it wasn't the first time he's met with them. But he's not the only one that's reported something like that to the commissioners the last few months. Other ranchers have done the same thing."

"I'm almost afraid to ask this, but have you found out anything more about who shot Ward the first time? Or anything about Lancaster?"

East shook his head. "Not a thing. We're calling the Lancaster case closed since it's almost certain that Ward shot him. And I guess it'll go down as Lancaster being the one that shot Ward, the first time anyway. I guess you could say that both cases are closed, and it's a good thing."

Jesse rolled a smoke. "Why's that?" he asked after he touched a match to the cigarette.

"We're going to be so damned busy serving arrest warrants that we wouldn't have time to investigate much anyway. The grand jury met this morning, too, and handed down a lot of indictments."

"I know the answer without asking," said Jesse, "but I don't reckon J. W. Cain's name was on one of those warrants?"

East grinned and shook his head and then both men were silent again. Jesse blew a cloud of gray smoke into the air and watched it spread. "Jim, I know you, but I don't know Garrett. Is he dealing cards to everybody from the same deck?"

The sheriff studied a minute, looked intently at the cigarette he was making. "Pat's a funny feller," he said at length, "but I think he's on the up and up. I don't think he came here to be anybody's chore boy.

He enforces the law like he sees it, and it just so happens that he sees it in the same way the Cattlemens' Association does. Which don't make it wrong, Jesse, in spite of what you think."

"And don't necessarily make it right either, does it?"

East stood up. "Hell, Jesse, I haven't got the time to discuss the finer points of law with you. I don't even know the finer points. You don't need to be a Philadelphia lawyer to be a sheriff in a cowtown. I'm not telling you right from wrong, I'm just telling you the way it is."

Coldiron took a deep breath, nodded, and gently rapped the desk top. "You're right, Jim, and I appreciate it, too. Like I said, I never doubted but what you were leveling with me; I was just wondering about Garrett. Did you send for him when the rustling got out of hand?"

"Oh, I didn't send for him, but I can't say I'm not glad he's here. I guess the Panhandle Cattlemens' Association sent for him. If Garrett and his men have an official name I guess it's the Home Rangers, but most people just call 'em the LS Rangers. The way that name got started is because Mr. Lee and his manager—the same J. E. McAllister that's one of the county commissioners—seem to be running the show. I don't mean telling Garrett who to arrest—like I said I don't think anybody could do that. What I mean and what rumor says—and if you ever tell anyone I told you this I'll call you a liar—is that the LS Ranch is paying him, and paying him good. One story has it that they're forking out over four hundred dollars a month to him and selling him cattle at below market value. My twenty-five a month don't stack up too high against that, does it?

"But Pat ain't never said a word to me about who sent for him or who's paying him, and as long as he does his job I don't figure it's any of my business. And considering the caliber of men he's been forced to hire, I'll have to admit he's doing a hell of a job."

Jesse adjusted his hat and turned toward the door. "Thanks for the palavering, Jim. I reckon I'd better let you get on home and eat supper." He stopped at the door and turned to face the sheriff again. "I guess Garrett and his men will be trying to find my cattle now, eh?"

East stood, slipped on his coat and hat and walked outside with Jesse. "Not likely, Jesse. Remember that Pat's first priority is to members of the Cattlemens' Association and in particular to the LS—for whatever reason, maybe it's just because they're the biggest and have lost the most cattle. I think he'd ride through hell and half of Iowa to get one LS pot-gutted dogie that he thought had been stolen, but he probably wouldn't cross a cow trail to pick up some of these cattle that are wearing another brand, even if that brand had been outlawed by the county."

The sheriff watched as Jesse swung a leg over the cantle of the worn-out saddle on Jug's back. When the cowboy was settled, East said, "Well, Jesse, I hope you find your cattle before anybody else does. I wish I could help."

"Thanks, Jim. I think somebody has already found 'em, though."

Jesse let Jug take his slow-walking time in going down Main Street and to the North Star Cafe. He had some thinking to do. J. W. Cain was certainly a lot of things not associated with neighborly, salt-of-the-earth folks. But he was good at what he did. *Exactly* what he did was still not entirely clear, but Jesse had a lot better hunch now than he did when he had ridden into town. When his morning coals hissed as the river water choked the life out of them he had thought Cain was a low-down, rotten, loud-mouthed, woman-bothering, cold-blooded killer and cattle thief. Now, as night hovered over the little river-bottom cattle town, he realized that J. W. Cain *was* all of those things—but not only those. After leaving Jim East he knew that Cain's account could not be closed out without adding some additional items to his ledger, debit side. The new entries included lying, conniving, scheming, calculating, and politicking.

Cain and his merry band of Christian souls were in the cattle-stealing business, not much doubt about that. But Cain was careful of what cattle he stole. He knew that if he stole from the big outfits they would sooner or later bring a noose down around his scheming neck, but if he took from the little man and the nobodies like Jesse he might just keep getting richer and more powerful.

Whenever he had some cattle that wore a brand that was not known around Tascosa he would go to the commissioners and tell them some cock-and-bull yarn and have the brand outlawed. That was just a precautionary measure to insure him against trouble if he were caught driving cattle not wearing his brand. All he had to do was say that he was gathering the grass-stealing trespassers up in order to turn them over to the county. If he wasn't caught with the herd it would wind up at his New Mexico ranch.

In Jesse's estimation the big outfits wouldn't give a

tinker's damn what Cain did with the cattle as long as they were out of the country and not using precious Panhandle grass to make their cud.

"A cowbird," Jesse said to no one, "picking bugs off a fat cow's back. As long as he don't pick in the wrong place, he's got it made."

CHAPTER 12

There was only one person in the North Star Cafe when Jesse opened the door. That person was Tracey James, beautiful, black-eyed, full-bosomed. She was setting the table in preparation for the evening's customers who would begin coming in with the half-hour.

Tracey looked up, said "Hello," and then went on about her work.

Jesse hung his hat on the hatrack by the door, said "Howdy," walked to a long table and sat down.

Tracey disappeared into the kitchen.

After a few minutes had passed she came back into the long dining room carrying a small pot. She filled the thick-glass cup in front of Jesse and sat the pot on the table.

"Thank you," Jesse said.

"Are you ready to eat?" Tracey asked formally.

After a few seconds Jesse said, "No."

Tracey walked around the end of the table, bound

for the kitchen once again. "When you're ready let me know."

As she was about to disappear through the door Jesse said, "I'm not going to eat."

She stopped and turned toward him. "Then why . . ."

"I'm not going to eat until you help me empty this coffee pot."

She said nothing, but neither did she continue on into the kitchen. She stood in the doorway, nervousness written in the graceful lines of her face. She turned her head enough to see out one of the windows beside the door. She looked across the street and at the long shadows of the late afternoon.

At long last Tracey spoke. "I don't drink coffee . . . but I try to eat before people start coming in. I could fill our plates in the kitchen . . . that is, unless you're still not ready to eat."

"Yes ma'am, that would be okay."

Tracey smiled as she leaned across the table to pick up the clean empty plate in front of the cowboy. And it was a real smile, not a faint one like Jesse had seen on the outskirts of town nine days ago, and not a strained, knowing one like he had seen in the graveyard two hours ago.

The steak wasn't the best he had eaten, but that aside, the meal had been as good as any he could remember. After Tracey had brought out the plates, they had eaten the first several bites in silence. But even in the silence both could tell that something had changed. The grimness which accompanied their earlier encounters—and had been in the cafe only a few minutes earlier—was now absent and in its place was an easy sort of atmosphere.

The longer they sat next to each other, even in

silence, the easier and more relaxed it became. After a bit, they made small talk about the food, the weather, the condition of the streets, the noise from the saloon next door, even the age of Harlan Harrell. Tracey not only smiled but laughed a little, subdued though it was.

No sound had ever affected Jesse, for better or for worse, more than Tracey's happy voice. If he had not been smitten by her before, he was now. If the gloomy and troubled forbearance she had shown him before had not captivated him—which it had—then the emerging radiance she now exhibited did. Her eyes were no darker than they were before, but now they had a sparkling, polished, youthful vigor about them. If there was ever a thing to make a man forget seventy-three head of springing crossbred heifers, it was a smiling young woman in a waist-hugging calico dress who smelled as fresh as a cool breeze coming from a thundercloud on a hot August afternoon.

In countless sprees through forgotten cowtowns Jesse thought he had been touched by a woman in every way that skin stretched over lithesome fingers could accomplish. That is, until Tracey placed her hand on his hard shoulder as she poured his third cup of coffee.

If the cowboy under that woman-warm hand wondered if it lingered just a moment longer than it was obliged to for ordinary coffee pouring, he was not alone.

Whether that innocent shoulder-touch was mere accident or not, whether that soft, warm hand rested on the cowboy's shoulder longer than was necessary or not, to the man just stepping upon the porch and looking through the glass in the door it could just as well have been a long, ardent embrace. Either way, J. W. Cain's eyes would not have stopped boring until they were hilt-deep in the cowboy's back.

Cain's big form filled the doorway and then stepped over the threshold. He was followed by two of the men Jesse had stood by at the bar of the Edwards Saloon, the shorter, bucktoothed one and the cadaverous-looking Slim. The trio momentarily halted as they entered the building, which was lighted only, and now insufficiently, by the barest remnants of tree-filtered daylight.

Jesse and Tracey had not noticed that the room was growing dimmer and dimmer as they ate and talked. They had been totally unaware of the fast approach of night as long as it was just the pair of them in the room. But they were suddenly aware of it now, and it was not just because the sun had slid out of sight. When the three men walked in a pall fell over the room that no amount of coal-oil light could drive away.

Tracey knew full well the reason behind the abrupt change and held her breath that what she feared would not come to pass. That Cain would find some way to let Jesse know that he regarded her as his, and why he did so, was her fear. That Cain would eat in dour silence or that Jesse, having finished his meal, would quickly leave, was her hope.

Jesse could account for the enmity between himself and the pompous, overbearing man pulling out a chair at the far end of the table. What he could not account for was the dread that had seized Tracey the moment Cain walked in. Did she suspect that he had caused Ward's death? Even if she did, her attitude toward him would be one laced with anger and not the fear that Jesse read in her face. And what about the day he heard them arguing? The broken plate? Jim East's remark about "something" between them?

When the three men sat down Tracey left the room. Cain pushed his hat back and looked at Jesse. "Coldiron," he said and nodded his head. It was recognition of his presence, nothing more.

"Cain," Jesse said, dry as a salt flat.

The door opened then and two more men, strangers to Jesse, came in and sat at the long dining table between him and the other three. Before these two had gotten settled in their chairs another man entered and sat opposite Jesse.

Tracey emerged from the kitchen and lit the three brass-bowl hanging lamps around the room and the two flat-wicks on the table, giving a soft yellow color to the room, but doing nothing to lessen the strain that was weighing heavily upon it.

The three newest patrons spoke a formal and rigid greeting to Cain and his men and then engaged in easygoing, cow-country talk. Mr. Sheets's voice could be heard coming from the kitchen along with the clanging of pans and the clinking of glass.

"The weather shore has purttied up after that first go-round of winter," said the man opposite Jesse.

"Yeah, agreed another, "an' I'll betcha we pay for it, too."

"Say, Bill," yet another said, "where's that little brother of yorn. I ain't seen him 'round lately."

"By gosh," said a man who must've been Bill, "he hired on with a fencing crew at Buffalo Springs. They're s'posed to start stringing fence for the XIT pretty soon. I heard they're going to put a outside fence plumb around that outfit."

Tracey was busy carrying bowls of potatoes, beans, gravy, and steak to the table. She was careful to avoid anyone's eyes, but Jesse thought her rigid manner had eased a little with the addition of the other customers to the table.

It seemed easier, that is, until Cain said to her, "You sure look pretty tonight, Tracey."

At Cain's words, congenial enough on the surface, Jesse saw her face pale, her eyes lose their new-found luster.

Cain wasn't through. "Don't she look pretty tonight, Coldiron?" He winked at Slim and grinned.

Jesse said nothing. He sipped his coffee and set the cup down without looking up, drew a vein-bulging hand down from his nose, over his mustache and off his set chin, but he said nothing.

The other men were alerted now to the chill in the air. They stopped their casual talk and ate in silence.

J. W. Cain made a mistake. He took the silence of Jesse Coldiron as a sign of weakness and cowardice. He was exhilarated by the thought that he had so easily buffaloed the cowboy in front of Tracey, and the other men, and had done it so fully.

Even had he not been so engrossed with himself, he would have probably failed to recognize the look on the face of the cowboy in the faded Levi's and threadbare shirt. The other men at the table might have known it. Men who had spent years following a trail herd or living with a chuck wagon on one big outfit or another would have known that look. It was no different than the look any cowpuncher worthy of the name wore when he bailed his cinch into a bronc's belly on a frosty morning and felt the horse draw up "tighter than a fiddle string"; when he untracked him before mounting and saw that he walked on tiptoes and that the back of his saddle was high enough to roll a watermelon under. The puncher would know that the bronc was going to pitch like hell, but by the look on his face—like the look on Jesse's now—the other cowboys could tell that he was going to "get his air tested."

Tracey brought a blackened pot out of the kitchen, steaming with freshly boiled coffee. Cain held up his cup for a refill, and as she poured he said, "You think she's pretty now, Coldiron, you ought to see the little red birthmark she has right there." As he said the last word he reached a hand up and touched her midway between her right shoulder and breast.

At his touch, Tracey recoiled and hurled the steaming pot in his direction in one lightning-swift motion. The pot ricocheted off the table top and overturned, spilling its scalding contents in Cain's lap. He only had time to jump to his feet and split the air with a single vile epithet before a spurred blur came hurling at him from the far end of the table, struck him chest-high, and slammed his heavy body against the wooden floor in a breath-robbing collision.

There was a flurry of sliding chairs and overturned bowls. Both men regained their feet. Before the bigger man could curl his hands into weapons, two granite-hard fists struck his face. One blow cut him above the left eye and the other brought blood from the corner of his mouth. He rocked backwards but was not floored.

Jesse closed quickly to strike again before Cain could recover, but not in time. A fist that carried two-hundred-thirty pounds behind it slammed into his face and sent him backwards and down, spitting blood.

With Jesse on the floor Cain snarled and landed a booted, but glancing, kick to his back. As the big foot drew back to deliver a second blow Jesse reached out an arm, grabbed a chair, and thrust it in the path of the oncoming boot.

Cain's foot struck the chair on the rungs and man and splintered chair fell to the floor with a crash.

Before the bigger man could regain his feet Coldiron was on top of him. Slinging fists like an out-of-control paddle wheel, Jesse landed two, three blows to the cheekbones beneath him before an iron-hard fist struck him in the chest, shot all the air out of his lungs and his body across the floor.

Out of the corner of his eye, Jesse saw Slim pull iron and heard the sickening metallic click of a .45 coming to full cock. The last click was drowned out by a deafening roar, followed by an ear-ringing silence broken only by the belated sound of breaking glass.

Tracey was standing beside the kitchen door, holding a ten-gauge, double-barreled shotgun that looked as big as a six-pound cannon. The shotgun was at her shoulder, and she was looking straight down the twin barrels of Damascus steel at Slim, who held the cocked Colt in his hand.

The right barrel of the shotgun was exhaling a thin ribbon of blue smoke that was drifting toward a fist-sized hole in the glass of the door. The left barrel was clear, waiting in front of its own cocked hammer.

"Get out," Tracey said flatly.

Cain stood, taking his time. He dusted himself off, wiped at the blood dripping from his chin with a handkerchief, and gingerly touched his lacerated cheek. "Coldiron," his tone was almost happy, "you're the deadest son of a bitch I know."

Cain's grave-cold eyes then locked on the slim figure holding the smoking shotgun. He spoke as if there were no one else in the room. "I'll be seeing you, Tracey." He paused, and wiped at his cheek again. Before he walked out of the North Star he said, "I mean real soon."

CHAPTER 13

Jesse stepped out of the cafe and looked at the vacant hitching post. Jug wasn't there of course. He had not expected him to be; the blast from the shotgun had spooked all the horses tied there. The big brown was standing on the other side of the street, nosing a little blue roan that was tied in front of the surveyor's office. The only good thing that had happened was that his bridle reins were not broken.

November had given way to December in no discernible way four days earlier, and December night air on the high plains is always cold, regardless of the days. The sharp air smelled of stabled horses and damp rotting leaves. In July, it would have been stifling. In late fall, it was refreshing, especially to a hot and sweaty Jesse Coldiron.

Jesse was in the saddle when he saw Sheriff East come from between two adobe buildings and hurry toward the North Star.

When East saw the street was empty except for a

single mounted cowboy sitting quietly in the saddle, he relaxed and walked up to him.

"What happened?" he asked Jesse. He was carrying his own shotgun but held it casually in one hand.

"Oh, hell, nothing much," Jesse said in his usual easygoing manner, "me and Cain just got into a little discussion and Tracey thought we oughta change the subject before it got outa hand."

"Who fired the shot?"

"Oh, hell, that was just ol' Cain shooting off his big mouth."

East looked across the dark street. The hole in the glass of the door to the North Star was easy to see. "And I guess that's what happened to that door, eh?"

"Why, yeah, sure," Jesse said as if he could not believe that East could have thought otherwise.

"And that swelling eye of yours? And that blood on your face?"

"Yeah." Jesse grinned.

East looked hard at the slim cowboy in the saddle, then walked toward the cafe.

"Jim," said Jesse before the sheriff had taken two steps, "I paid Sheets for the damages. Cain went his way, and now I'm going mine."

"See that you do that, Jesse. If you don't keep riding and not come back, you're apt to get yourself killed."

Jesse rode away and stuck a hand up to acknowledge his friend's statement. But heed it he did not.

He turned Jug south at the first corner, rode past a few adobe houses scattered across three blocks, stopped two hundred yards past the last house, and dismounted on a grassy bank of the river.

Hobbling Jug, Jesse washed the blood and battle dirt from his face and hands. He then untied the saddle strings that secured his coat to the back of his saddle, put it on, sat in the grass, and pulled out his Bull Durham.

He slowly rolled a cigarette, stopping often to think about what had happened since he walked into the cafe a short while ago. One thing for sure, he wasn't sorry about the fight. If he ever saw anybody that was overdue for an eyedotting it was J. W. Cain.

Jesse finished the first cigarette and rolled a second. As he smoked, he lay on one elbow with his head in his hand and listened to the timeless sounds of autumn. A coyote howled far, far away. An unseen flight of geese overhead honked their way south. A few crickets, somehow surviving the blizzard, chirped in the grass.

A smile grew on his face as he thought about the meal—and the smiles, and friendly talk, and the touch of a warm hand—that he and Tracey had shared before the storm broke. If he was sorry about anything it was that Tracey's smiling face would be harder to get out of his mind than her sad one had been. Somehow, he had a feeling that, in spite of the few minutes of happiness they had known, his actions would end up bringing her more trouble and sadness.

Jesse tossed his cigarette butt into the river and stretched out on his back, hands behind his head, looking at the brightening points of light in the clear, black, moonless sky. A night like Tracey's eyes, he thought. What was it between her and Cain? Surely, he didn't know anything about a birthmark under her dress. Did he? How could he? He just touched her there and said that to get him stirred up. Well, that he accomplished with rip-roaring success. But he could have done that in a lot of other ways, none of which would have embarrassed the prettiest woman in town. It didn't figure. . . .

Coldiron froze. Jug perked up his ears and looked in the direction of town. They both had heard the snap of a dry twig. Jesse watched Jug out of the corner of his eye and eased his hand downward until it touched the cold butt of his Colt. The .45 crept out of its holster. By watching Jug, Jesse knew that whoever was sneaking up on him was just now at the edge of the cottonwoods and would be silhouetted against the lights of town.

Bunching his muscles for action, he rolled over and brought the .45 to full cock. The instant he was on his belly both hands were on the butt of the heavy gun and his right forefinger was flattening out and turning white from its pressure on the trigger.

"Jesse! Don't!" said Tracey in an excited, frightened voice.

Circulation returned to Jesse's trigger finger. He lowered the hammer carefully. "Good God, Tracey!" Jesse said with an escape of breath. He lay still another moment, more scared than when he thought someone was going to try to kill him. "I thought you were Cain and his bunch."

He stood and watched the Colt slide back into its holster. "How did you know I was down here?"

"I was just looking down toward the river, thinking. When I saw the flare of a match I had an idea it was you."

"Well, it's a good thing it was me. You took a pretty big chance."

"And you did, too, Jesse. That's why I wanted to see you again. . . . to thank you."

"I don't know what for," said Jesse, "all I did was probably make more trouble for you. I hope your boss isn't too mad."

"Never mind about that. It was worth anything to see Cain down on that floor."

"Yeah," Jesse said, "you shoulda seen his eyes just before I hit him."

"I did." Tracey laughed a little. "I saw his face just about the time you were over the table." Tracey now laughed a little harder. "His eyes got as big as the bowl of potatoes you knocked off. I never saw anybody so surprised in my life."

Her laugh was infectious. Jesse pictured what she was saying and began to chuckle himself, saying, "I wonder what he was thinking?"

Tracey sat in the thick grass beside the river, holding her skirt in place and stretching out her legs. She leaned back on her arms and laughed, not a loud laugh but a soft feminine one.

Jesse sat beside her, his shoulders giving away his laughter. "It must've been a heck of a shock to a man as important as he thinks he is to have someone pour hot coffee on him and then have somebody else knock him flat."

"I wish you could have seen yourself," Tracey said, her laugh still feminine but louder, "sitting on top of him in the middle of the floor slinging your arms like a little boy riding a barrel."

Their laughter released the tension, anger, and fear that had built during the brief but violent fight. Once started laughing, they could not stop. What had been so savage and frightening a short while ago, now became hilariously funny. Ludicrously funny. Everything said now became a new reason to laugh. Finally, with tears in their eyes, they gave up trying to talk and just lay back in the grass and laughed.

The laughing quieted and slackened. Then it came only in spasms, sandwiched between the chirping of the crickets and the honk of the geese. Then it died out entirely. They lay still and silent and exhausted—and happy.

They lay there for some time—neither knew nor cared how long—content to share the passing moments and the other's presence without having to justify their lingering. Whoever it was that said silence was golden must have had in mind a sun-cured, hard-baked cowboy and a doe-skinned, raven-haired young woman surrounded by a dark autumn hush.

After a while, Tracey sat up and rubbed at the goose bumps under the long sleeves of her cotton dress. Jesse slipped his coat over her shoulders in silence.

As his hands fell on her shoulders she turned to him. It wasn't a planned turn, but instinctive, done without foreknowledge. With no conscious command from him, his hands pulled her gently closer. In the almost total darkness her face was barely visible, yet he could see the softness of her lips.

And then, that which would have seemed as unlikely fifteen days earlier as a world in which stones rolled uphill, came to pass.

In spite of all the odds to the contrary, they kissed. Their lips met not in passion, but in hesitation. Not out of desire, but out of a longing that neither had been able, nor willing, to admit before that moment.

Their lips had been together for no longer than it

takes a shooting star to flare and die when Tracey turned her face away and said in a soft, sad voice, "Jesse . . . we can't . . . I can't." And then she stood, turned her back to him and started walking away.

Jesse stepped behind her, put his hand on a shoulder of hers and stopped her. She twisted out from under his hand and said, "Jesse, no! No more. Please."

"Tracey," Jesse said behind her. "I . . ."

"Jesse, I've got to tell you about . . . about . . ." Suddenly, she broke into a sobbing run. Jesse caught her in two long strides, grabbed an arm only to have it jerked away.

This time he didn't run after her. In two quick steps she had shed the coat, in three she had vanished into the darkness that stretched between the river and town.

In however many steps it took for her to cover half the distance to the North Star Cafe, that's how many she took before she stopped. She was gasping for breath, tasting salty tears, and the black bun at the back of her head was coming unpinned—but none of these things had caused her to stop.

She was standing between two dark-windowed adobe houses that were two hundred yards apart. Her mind was still racing as fast as her feet had been a moment ago. A shaggy cur dog yapped at her from twenty feet away. She was close enough to Main Street to have easily heard the shouts, music, giggles, and shrieks coming from there. But she didn't hear any of it, not the barking dog, not the saloon noise. Somewhere between where she now stood and where she and Jesse had shared one tender kiss, came the realization that she had an obligation to him. As she dried her eyes and tried to straighten her hair, her mind was already making plans to fulfill that obligation. Time was short, however. She had to have those plans finalized, drawn up and laid out before she retraced her steps back to the river.

In his easygoing manner, Jesse had made her smile, even laugh, and he had made her feel alive and like a woman again. Those things hadn't happened to her in a long, long time. And he had done something else that she had never seen anyone do—stand up to J. W. Cain.

Those were three of the facts she was examining as she made her way by the starlight down a well-worn trail that connected the river and the town. But, important as those three facts were to Tracey, they were by no means the only ones on her mind. The fourth fact—and it was receiving a disproportionate amount of examination time—was that she loved Jesse Coldiron. Maybe she had known it before, but she would never have admitted it then. Then, she had been afraid, even ashamed, of the feelings that he stirred in her whenever he was near. Now, she knew those feelings were natural and that love could have no shame in it.

As she followed the trail around a small growth of cholla cactus, she thought of the fifth—and final—fact, and the flush that had come to her face while thinking about the kiss was suddenly gone, and she had to stop. It needed no examining. It was uncontestable. It was the root of the obligation she had and the reason the plan had been devised.

J. W. Cain would kill Jesse, and all because of her.

Therein lay the obligation. She owed it to Jesse to give him no reason to stay in Tascosa or to see her again.

And therein, also, lay the plan. She would make Jesse think that she cared nothing for the likes of him.

She could feel the tears start to build in her eyes again. Her bottom lip quivered. She *had* to control herself now because she was getting near the river. If her plan was to succeed, she had to be strong. She even had to be cold and hard. She had practiced those two traits for a long time, and with much success, but they would not come so easily now. Not with Jesse.

"Jesse," said Tracey, standing near the end of the trail, "it's me, you're not going to try to shoot me again, are you? Where are you? I can't see a thing."

"I'm just a little ways in front of you. Just come on down the trail."

In a few short steps she was beside the river. Jesse was sitting on the same bank where they were earlier.

"Where did you run off to, Tracey? Why . . ."

"I'm sorry," she said, laughing, "but you seemed to think that it was something other than what it was, and I get nervous when men do that."

She could only see a dark outline on the ground where he was, which was for the better.

"And what was it?" he asked.

"A kiss, Jesse. Period. One playful kiss that meant nothing at all."

In an easy voice Jesse said, "Is that all it was?"

Tracey tossed her head back and laughed a coarse and vulgar laugh, at least one as coarse and vulgar as she could manage. "You cowboys really get me," she said. "You're all just alike. Jesse, do you really think that you're the first man I've met down here at the river? And you're no different from the others.

One kiss or pat on the knee and you start imagining all kinds of things that aren't so.''

Jesse's reply was the same as it always was—slow in coming and laconic when it arrived. "I don't remember imagining nothing, Tracey."

"Well, good. I'd better get back to my room. I'm expecting company pretty soon. I just came back to make sure you didn't get any stupid ideas about that kiss. Like, thinking that you were the man I'd been waiting for all my life. Or, that I was dying to spend the rest of my life on a broken-down ranch in the middle of nowhere with you, having your babies.''

"Naw," the cowboy drawled. He was finding pebbles now and thumbing them one at a time into the river. His voice suddenly seemed much farther away than it was, and it sounded, at least to Tracey, as lonesome as the night wind whistling through a deserted house. "I didn't figure nothing like that. Shoot, I know a man like me couldn't ever give a woman like you what you oughta have. And it's plain as the dickens to see that you're too pretty of a woman to grow old out in the middle of nowheres with some cowboy.''

Jesse grew quiet then, the world grew quiet, except for an occasional pebble making a weak splash.

Tracey's lips quivered. A silent tear fell in the grass at her feet.

"But, Tracey," Jesse said after an eternity, each word measured and slow, "if I ever amount to anything someday . . . I'll be back. And I'll build you the best house you ever saw. And I'll see to it that you have everything you ever wanted. And you won't owe me anything, Tracey. Not even one playful kiss.''

That was where the plan fell through.

Tracey leaned against a lone tree and cried. When Jesse came to her and held her in his arms he said, "It looks like it's time we quit sidling off from whatever this thing is that's ahold of you and head straight into it."

CHAPTER 14

And they did. They backed up and hit *it* head-on, square in the middle, right there by the river, sitting in the grass, she in his coat, a blanket taken from behind the cantle of Jesse's saddle around both, she leaning back into his arms, he smelling the fragrance of her long, let-down hair, with Jug clipping away at the riverbank grass.

Tracey, although her voice faltered now and again, never sidled once. Nor did she mince her words; she told him everything in as short and unflattering a way as possible.

Her story amounted to two lecherous scoundrels, both of vulgar free will and with shameless knowledge aforethought, taking wanton advantage of a beautiful eighteen-year-old girl, pure and chaste but frightened and alone.

Scoundrel number one came into her life only a few weeks after her father had been murdered while on a hide-buying trip among the many buffalo-hunter camps near Mobeetie. Tracey had always been beautiful, but she now also suddenly became alone, frightened, vulnerable, the sole support for a young brother—all things the scoundrel was well aware of. He courted her, bought her expensive gifts . . .

In short, the beautiful quarter-Indian slip of a girl found herself serving drinks in the establishment where this gentleman dealt cards.

Lying in bed with him later, he swore his love to her until the last card should slip from his fingers. For some reason, Tracey took this to mean that he would love her until his death. How was she to know that in his parlance "the last card" was the one he carried up his sleeve, and that if it "slipped from his fingers" he could stand to lose a bundle?

Ere long, he didn't lose just *a* bundle, but rather he lost his *whole* bundle. And not only that, he owed *another* bundle to two very close-eyed buffalo skinners, both of whom kept their skinning knives razor sharp.

Enter scoundrel number two. He was a man almost as big as a buffalo, and more dangerous. He was, perhaps, the worst of a whole passel of hard-cores who made their livings off the men who made their livings off the buffalo. But he possessed a certain flair that the other rogues lacked. He was able to get the less astute to do the dirty work while he sat in the saloons or gambling houses and maintained his well-coiffured appearance. He was a self-styled connoisseur with a special penchant for fine food, liquor, and women.

As scoundrel number one's dangerous predicament rapidly deteriorated and the odds on his reaching old age fell from a nervous "about even" to a nail-biting "forget it," scoundrel number two, with inscrutable timing, came charging to his rescue. This savior of scoundrel one's, this paragon of modesty and humility, of course, was J. W. Cain.

The part that followed—the solution to the gambler's problem—was the most loathsome.

The plan the two chivalrous souls agreed upon was a simple one, and—except for the particulars—ageless. It involved a merchandising scheme that has been practiced with minor variations since the lowlands were still ankle deep in waters left from the Flood— trading in young women. Their particular contract read thus: Cain would liquidate the gambler's debt, and in return, said gambler would see to it that Cain's sheets were pressed by the softest, warmest, most desirable, tan-skinned, black-haired, ripe-breasted girl in the Township of Mobeetie, County of Wheeler, State of Texas.

And on top of that, said girl would come to his bed willingly. Why? Because scoundrel number one would convince her that she should. He could do it. He swore to Cain he could.

But Tracey said no. Never. *Why not?* he demanded. Why did he think? she replied. *Would she rather see him dead? Was that all he meant to her?* Of course not, but there had to be another way. *Well, there wasn't. It was either that or else he was a dead man.* She had an answer: They could leave town! *And go where? They wouldn't get two miles before some buffalo hunter saw them and relayed the word to the two after his hide.* But there HAD to be another way. They'd just have to look until they found it. *Well, she'd have to find it herself, because by the next morning he'd be dead.* Look, it wasn't like he was *asking her to live with the man or anything. Good God, she wouldn't be in there over a couple of hours. Surely, for two hours she could . . . surely, for him she could . . .* Okay. Okay. THIS time and NO more. He had to promise her that. No more. Ever.

So, the disgusting contract was going to be discharged that very evening. The trouble was, what the girl in the long black hair and the stunning figure capitulated to, and what the charitable J. W. Cain understood would be executed in his room, were not the same thing.

She had not asked exactly how much it was that her man owed, or how much J. W. Cain was going to be out for his part of the deal. If she had known that, she would have known that no man would pay that amount for what *she* thought was going to happen. She thought she would have supper with him in his room, wear the same clothes she wore to the saloon, smile a lot, maybe dance with him. Something like that.

"Jesse," she said, five years after the fact, "as hard as it is to believe now, I *really* thought that was all I was going to that room for. I know it's hard to believe that anybody could have been that dumb, but right then there was nobody, anywhere, any dumber than I was." She hesitated a few seconds then continued.

"When I got to his room, he was standing over by a window. He just looked at me and smiled and told me to come stand beside him. I tried to smile, like I was supposed to, but I already had a sickening feeling about what he seemed to have in mind.

"But there I was, and I did what he said and went over to where he was. When I did, he grabbed me and kissed me and his hands were going everywhere!

I broke loose, but he just reached out one big hand and held me like a vice. Before I knew what was happening he had the top of my dress unbuttoned.

"I jerked loose and nearly made it to the door before he caught me again. He said, 'Come 'ere, you're already bought and paid for. You're supposed to help me, but I don't care, all a little wrestling does is to get the blood pumping good.'

"He picked me up. . . . threw me on the bed. Then he grabbed my dress at the waist and just ripped it off, mashed me down on the bed with one hand and tore off the rest of what clothes were still on. Everything. *It happened so fast!* I was beating on his back with my fist, but I know he didn't even feel it. With him on top of me I could hardly breathe, much less move.

"It's been five years, Jesse, and sometimes I wake up at night thinking that I can still feel his hands on me, especially since he found me again.

"Anyway just when there seemed to be no way . . . just before he . . . My left hand felt a washbowl on the bedstand; I twisted my head around and saw a razor by the bowl. I grabbed it and rammed the end of it in his back, not the blade, the other end. He felt it enough to raise up a little, but when he did he just laughed. When he started back down I jabbed the razor between us and sliced at his face!"

Tracey shivered in Jesse's arms in spite of the blanket and the coat.

"I felt the razor scrape against his cheekbone. The muscle on his face just opened up, I could see the bone, but it didn't start bleeding for a second or two. He shot up, grabbed his face with both hands, and I rolled off the bed. I was naked, but I didn't even think about that. I *had* to get out of there! I ran down the hall, across the lobby, and down the street to where Ward and I lived—I didn't care who saw me, I just had to get home."

She told Jesse there was no shortage of stories around Mobeetie during the next few days about what exactly went on that night in Cain's room. The gambler and the two skinners disappeared, never to be heard from again. Some claimed to have seen their carcasses rotting alongside some of the thousands of naked, bloated dead buffalo that littered the prairie nearby; others had them alive and healthy in various points on the map nowhere near Wheeler County. Those who knew the disposition of J. W. Cain doubted that any were alive.

It was never entirely clear whether there was a conspiracy between the skinners and the gambler, or whether the gambler was just playing both sides against the middle.

Her tale almost complete, Tracey stood up, took a few steps, and stopped immediately at water's edge. She looked across its width but the moonless night hid the opposite shore.

"Soon after that happened," she said quietly but with no bitterness, no self-pity, "I found out I was pregnant. I kept my job at the saloon for a while because Ward and I had to eat, but when I started showing I was fired. It wasn't easy, but we survived. Ward was old enough to do a few odd jobs around town; he could have gone out with the skinners, but I wasn't about to let him do that, not as young as he was. Sometimes it was handouts or nothing, but we survived.

"As soon as Nina was born I tried getting a job in the mercantiles and the cafes, but any time it looked like I might get one, the man's wife would show up, give him a big frown, and all of a sudden he decided he couldn't afford any help. I didn't blame them any; everyone in town knew about me: former saloon girl, running down the street naked, the mother of an illegitimate baby. No, I couldn't fault them. The trouble was, they knew *about* me, they didn't *know* me.

"Anyway, I was determined that we wouldn't live on handouts again, that we would make it on our own. As long as we were in Mobeetie—and we couldn't afford to leave—there was just one place I could work. As soon as my figure came back I went back to work at the saloon. But I wasn't the same girl that I was the first time I put on black stockings and a low-cut dress—I was a lot wiser. I had learned the hard way about the world, and about men. I smiled when I had to, but that was *all* any man ever got from then on. I wasn't interested in their little games, their dirty talk, or their money. And I told more than one that same thing.

"Cain's face healed after a few weeks. But his pride never did. I used to catch him looking at me in the saloon, and I could tell what he was thinking. Twice he told me that when I got hungry enough I would be in his room, that I knew where it was, then he would grab my arm and tell me that the first time was already paid for and to not ever forget it. Once, when I got home from the saloon and struck a match to light the lantern he was there, just sitting there in the dark waiting for me. He asked me if I knew why no men were 'after' me. I told him because that was the way I wanted it. He called me a stupid little wench and said that it was because he had put out the word that I was his, and everyone knew better than to touch me. I thought then that he was going to . . . rape me. Maybe kill me. He said not to worry, that I would know when it was time, and then he left.

"Then one day Harlan's letter about the job at the North Star came. I used what money we had saved to pay a freighter who hauled supplies here to let us ride his wagon. We packed what little we had and left in the middle of the night without a word to anyone. We even walked out of town in the dark and met the freighter in the country. When we got here, the freighter said he would keep our secret, and I think he did. He wouldn't even let us pay him what we'd agreed on for bringing us.

"When we first got here, and for several months afterwards, I thought it was heaven. We all had a new life, a chance to start over. At least I knew a few mistakes *not* to make. But now? Ward and Nina don't have any life at all and my old one has caught up with me again."

After a short pause, Tracey got up and stood with her back to Jesse. She said pensively, "Now you know why I said it could go no farther for us. If we had met before . . . but what happened between us was a mistake. You see, I'm already spoken for, body . . . maybe even soul, too. Sometimes I think that he owns both and is just waiting until he's ready before claiming them. Anyway, I want you to know, Jesse, that you have *no* obligation to me, and I feel none toward you. It's time to go your way and I'll go mine."

She looked up at the sky, breathed deeply, and clasped the coat tighter about her. She felt the frigid air pinch her skin. Behind her, Jesse was silent. She wanted him to say something, yet was glad he did not. She fought back her tears. She wouldn't cry now, not here; he had seen the last of her tears. She wondered what he thought of her *now*. If only he had not come back to Tascosa, had never learned the awful truth.

She knew that now was the time to leave him—forever. As she steeled herself for that, she heard him stir. Without turning around, she knew he was standing close behind her.

"You're right," he said gently and with a voice saddened by grim reality, "about us going our own ways, but not for the reasons you said. All you did wrong in Mobeetie was to trust the wrong man. I've done worse a thousand times, Tracey. I've been with women that I forgot the names of as soon as the seat of my pants hit the saddle. If there's anybody that's got a past they ought to hate to tell, it should be me instead of you.

"But the past isn't why we have to go our own separate ways, it's the future. I could predict yours if you spend it with a cowboy like me—gray hair, early wrinkles, and faded flour-sack dresses."

Tracey turned to go straight toward town. They were both silent as she took the first step away from him. But while her logic was reeling off the reasons why it had to be, Tracey's feet were turning her around and carrying her into Jesse's arms. They had both just learned an age-old truth—love is no respecter of logic.

For the second time that evening, Tracey's lips and Jesse's came together. The first time, though, only their lips had touched. This time, their bodies pressed together in a passionate embrace. Tracey encircled the cowboy's waist with both arms and pulled him close. Jesse could feel the warmth of her body and the fullness of her breasts against him. Past and future were now both as forgotten as the murmuring river at their feet and the singing nightbird across its waters. They sank to the grass, still embracing.

Whatever would have happened in the grass from that point forward—whatever pleasures they would have given each other, how much love, and, perhaps, however much regret they would have known after their unbridled desires had been quenched—was never to be known, because they were interrupted by the sound of horses coming along the river and muffled voices as the riders approached.

Jesse and Tracey lay still on the grass, not daring to move nor speak. Jug stopped eating and lifted his head. He pointed his ears in the direction of the sounds but held his nicker.

The sounds coming to them out of the dark were as common in cow country as the bawl of a calf for its mother. They were everyday sounds that ordinarily would not have warranted so much as an absent-minded turn of the head. But not now. Now there was something menacing in the heavy fall of horses' hoofs, something sinister in the occasional jingle of spurs and bridles, and—when the horses stopped—something foreboding in the hushed tones in which the riders spoke.

What the men said was impossible for Jesse and Tracey to make out, so low did they speak. But when all sounds of horses and men suddenly ceased, Jesse tensed and his right hand left the soft skin of Tracey's neck and grasped the Colt revolver. He dared not risk cocking the hammer, but his thumb rubbed back and forth along its cold ear in anticipation.

After an eternity the sounds came again, this time they brought relief. Hoofs thumped, spurs jingled, saddle leather faintly creaked, and then all faded away, leaving only the sound of the river and the dim bark of a town dog.

After a few more moments of cautious silence, Jesse rolled to his feet and reholstered the Colt. As Tracey sat up, she said in a whisper, "Jesse, you have got to get out of here. Now!"

Without another word the cowboy walked to his horse. When he pulled the hobbles from Jug's forelegs he turned to Tracey and said, "Will you come with me?"

"Jesse, what? I don't . . . I can't . . . I mean . . ."

"Tracey," Jesse said. He stepped closer to her, holding his bridle reins in hand, "I know I don't have any right to ask you. And I know I don't deserve anybody as fine and pretty as you. And all I can promise you'll ever have is my love, but you'll have all of that forever, whether you go with me or not. Tracey, I know I'm not much of a hand at proposing but . . ."

"Jesse," Tracey interrupted with shock in her voice, "are you . . . are you asking me to marry you?"

"I am," said Jesse.

"Marry you? Jesse, we can't. . . . What about Cain?"

"Well," Jesse said with a certain happiness in his voice, "he was my second pick, thought I'd ask you first."

Tracey James, the young woman who had worked so hard for so long to show no emotion in anything she did or said, answered half-laughing and half-crying,

"Jesse Coldiron . . . I . . . Yes, Jesse, I would be proud to be your wife."

The next little while was spent in joyful haste. They were anxious to get out of town before J. W. Cain saw them but even more anxious about the event that would precede their departure. Tracey shed her cotton dress and slipped into her wedding clothes—which happened to be her riding clothes—denim britches and corduroy shirt. She plaited her thick mane into a single long braid and packed the few things she could not leave into a cloth bag. Into that bag she placed two cotton dresses and underclothes, a worn Bible, a faded daguerreotype of her father and mother, and a rag doll that had been her Nina's favorite. Meanwhile, Jesse had gone straight away to the livery stable two doors down and purchased a wedding gift for his bride—a twenty-dollar paint horse and a five-dollar saddle.

In three hours from the time Jesse had walked into the North Star Cafe, offered Tracey a nervous greeting and sat down at the long table, he was in the home of Scotty Wilson, Justice of the Peace. Seldom, if ever, has a courtship been shorter, a wedding held in a simpler setting, or a man and woman more in love and sure of what they wanted.

And though Jesse had to pay Scotty Wilson fifty cents extra for the words that went with the two-dollar marriage license, and though the words he said to them would have hardly been recognized as marriage vows by anyone else, to the lean cowboy and the beaming woman at his side, the vows were as sacred and binding as if repeated in the center of Zion with the Virgin Mother herself as witness.

When they stepped once again into the dark, cold outdoors, it seemed to them neither dark nor cold. They paused beside the horses just long enough for a long and tender wedding kiss before settling into their saddles for the thirty-mile ride to Minneosa Canyon.

of horses' hoofs on sandy soil, the louder report of a hard hoof striking rock, the sounds of the saddles, or the sounds of the prairie birds and animals around them. Regardless, they rode contented. Jesse had never seen a woman so at home on a horse or so unafraid of the untamed land through which they rode. She seemed to revel in its isolation and to be a part of its grandeur. With each breath of its sage-scented air she seemed to Jesse more alive, with each passing mile more at peace, and with each glance of his, more beautiful.

As for Tracey, she had never known a man as open and straightforward as Jesse; a man who could talk so little about love, yet by his mere presence and quiet glances, make her feel so loved and wanted. In town he had seemed a little smaller than he was, a little out of place; but out here he seemed as big as the stunning expanse of hills and dark-shadowed canyons that stretched away in all directions like an endless grass-covered ocean. Out here he and his horse moved in unison, and Jesse seemed as much a part of the rugged landscape as the dry creeks and the flowing springs.

She got the impression he could sense the mood of the land and understand its being. If he said there should be a spring along a certain draw, there was, as surely as if he had been there when it bubbled to life long ago. If he said he figured there should be a trail in a certain place, there was, as if he had been there when each of the tens of thousands of longhorn and buffalo hoofs hewed it out of the earth over hundreds of past seasons. He was in complete command, yet he commanded nothing—rather, as the earth exercised her will, he gracefully molded himself to fit her contour. Whatever hardships, heartaches, and mistakes were in Tracey's past, if but this—this one ride, these few hours—was all they purchased, she would know them well spent.

As she watched Jesse give Jug the rein to work his way down a steep, rocky hillside, she was suddenly seized with the desire to stop and consummate their marriage on the open prairie under a canopy of vibrant stars and pale moon, to be his wife in every sense of the word. For along with the utter joy and contentment of the moment lurked something else— the cold dispassionate nature of reality. That reality warned her that the clock marking their time together was not perpetual, but that it was running on a spring, a short spring, maybe to be wound but once.

When the horses leveled off again Tracey realized that they had just come off the rim of a canyon and were within its narrow confines. Then she smelled the mesquite smoke and the coffee coming from Harlan's dugout.

Harlan was up and pacing the floor of the dugout like a bronc on a short stake. When Jesse and Tracey rode around to the front of the dugout he was standing in the open doorway. "Coldiron," he said as if he were about to scold a wayward child, "where in the hell you been . . . ? Oh, Tracey . . . Well, how do ya do, girl." He studied the couple for a moment while both of them grinned at him. Finally, he returned the grin and said, "I can't say too much for the company you keep, Tracey, but it is a fact that it's good to see your pretty face."

Jesse leaned forward in the saddle with his forearms on the horn and flashed a teasing grin. "Mr. Harrell," he said. "I'd like for you to meet Mrs. Coldiron."

Quick as a slapping at a sweat bee, Harlan searched Jesse's face for a clue to the joke, found none and switched his gaze to the blushing woman. "Huh? Do what? Mrs. . . . What the . . . ?" he muttered in absolute and total disbelief, most of his smile intact, waiting for them to spring the punch line.

"Jesse and I were married a few hours ago," Tracey said softly, proudly, and with her face beaming so much that Harlan was forced to abandon his smile and accept the impossible, eyebrow-raising truth of what they were saying.

"Uh-huh. Mmmm," he said, more to himself than to either of them. He was turning the fact over and over in his mind and still finding no possible way for it to be anything but cockeyed. "Tracey," he said, his eyes on Jesse all the while, "why don't you come in and rest? You must be wore to a nub." Then growing gruffer he said, "Me an' Jesse will tend to the horses.

"All right, Coldiron," Harlan demanded as soon as Tracey had dismounted and walked into the dugout. "Suppose you tell me how in the hell it is you can leave here with nothing on your dim mind but finding seventy-three head a piggy heifers—and I mean *nothing* else, I most near had to force you to have a drink with me and you *said* you was obstinating from women 'cause you was celerbating—and then you come galavanting back in two days an' a piece with a wife! And not just *a* wife, hell no, but *the* sweetest, prettiest little girl in Texas that ain't got no more business taking up with the likes of you than a lady bug does a wart hog. Now just s'pose you tell me that, Mr. Cattle-Baron-That-Don't-Thank-About-Nothing-But-Cattle!"

Jesse was busy loosening the cinches on his saddle, taking his time. He was stalling and he knew it. "Well, Harlan, hell . . ."

"Yeah," interrupted his partner, "you can by God say that again. Hell! What woulda happened if you'd been looking for a hundred heifers, or two hundred, or by God what if it'd been a thousand? What would you've come back with then? The whole goddamn End of the World Hotel from Miles City. . . . But by God, Coldiron, that's what I mean, Tracey ain't like that! And I'll be damn . . ."

Jesse pulled the saddle off and rolled it under the lean-to. "Harlan, I know that Tracey ain't like . . ."

"Yeah!" Harlan said as he yanked the bit out of the mouth of Tracey's paint hard enough to level the long ridges on its teeth, "And I gotta know just how well do you know 'er. And," here Harlan lowered his voice and talked through clenched white teeth that got closer and closer to Jesse's face as he spoke, "I gotta know something else, Coldiron, and I gotta know 'er now. Are you still celerbating, and if you are, hows come you got married, and if you ain't, Coldiron, did you stop before or after them wedding vows was took! Huh? Well, come on, out with it, you rancid debacker!"

By now both Jug and the paint had been turned loose in the corral with Harlan's sorrel and Jesse's dun packhorse. Jesse threw an ample portion of mesquite beans over the fence and stood with an arm resting on a crooked cedar post, watching the horses eat and bicker over who was going to stand where. "Harlan," he said slowly, "I gotta lot to tell you."

"Jesse," the old man said, somewhat calmer than before, "that's gotta be the goddamnest underest statement ever said."

"Well, first off, I know who has our cattle."

"Do you now," Harlan said cockily. He swung his head from side to side. "I know *where* they are!"

Jesse jerked around. "You do? Where?"

"Aha! I reckon that'll have to keep for now. I'll tell you where they are after you tell me what's going on, what you're up to. And suppose you start with that little tan-skinned girl that just went in that dugout yonder."

Jesse lowered one knee to the ground, placed his crossed forearms on the other and leaned heavily on it. He lifted his head to look at the dugout and the dim light coming from it. He kept his voice low so Tracey couldn't hear from inside. There were a lot of things he could think of that he'd rather be doing than trying to explain to Harlan about him and Tracey, mainly because he could hardly explain it to himself, and he had heard her laugh, seen her cry, tasted her lips, and felt her skin.

"Harlan," he began, "you're not one whit more surprised at what's happened than I am, I can guarantee you that. When I left here the day before yesterday —hell, even seven or eight hours ago—if somebody would of wanted to bet me that I'd be married right now, I'd of bet every last one of them heifers and throwed in old Jug and the dun, to boot, I'd *never* be married."

Harlan pulled up a piece of earth next to the younger man and eased his stiff body to the ground. He sat cross-legged and for once was more interested in listening than talking. The moon had slid down the sky far enough so that they were almost in the shadow of the west canyon wall. The air was cold and windless, without so much as a blade of grass stirring. The horses chomped and crushed the dried beans in the corral behind them.

Jesse changed positions and sat down in the grass with his feet in front of him. "I didn't plan none of it," he said. "I just went into the North Star to eat supper with Tracey. Before I left J. W. Cain came in. We got into a little fisticuffs over what he said to Tracey, and what he did. After that, me and Tracey wound up down by the river."

Jesse grew silent, Harlan looked at him and prodded, "Yeah? And then what?"

"I asked her if she'd marry me. It was about that simple, but it's not that simple to explain it. All I know is that we just want to be together."

"Do you know about Cain? I mean *everything* about him?" asked Harlan.

"Yeah," affirmed Jesse, "Cain, the gambler, Nina, everything. None of it matters. She's the most decent woman I've ever known and I'd try to smother out the fires of Hell with my own hide if I thought she needed or wanted me to."

"Does this mean," asked Harlan intently, "that Jesse Coldiron is ready to settle down on a farm and raise kids?"

"No. All it means is that Jesse Coldiron and Tracey James are ready to spend the rest of their lives together. It doesn't mean that I cotton to the smell of fresh-plowed ground anymore now than I ever did. I've punched cows too long to change, and Tracey knows it. She says she just wants to go where I go. I know I haven't got anything to offer a woman like her, and it mighta been the dumbest thing in the world for us to get married. But from where we stand, as much as we want to be together, it would have been even dumber not to.

"There's just no way a man can understand what I'm talking about unless he's held a woman like her in his arms. I mean a real woman, Harlan. One as decent and downright beautiful as she is. And one that's in his arms because she wants to be and not because he's half drunk and in the mood to spend a month's wages in one night."

"Well, now, Mr. Coldiron," Harlan said with the gaiety returning to his voice, "maybe I didn't know you all these years as good as I thought I did. Smother out the fires of Hell, huh? Hee, hee. No, I sure as hell never figured you for that—feeding them fires, yeah; but smothering them?"

"Now, what about those heifers?" asked Jesse.

"I'll take you to see 'em first daylight, they ain't far. That's the good news. The bad news is that it'd take a whole regiment of Texas Rangers to get 'em back. Now, I'm going to talk to the bride; I've seen the groom's ugly face enough for one night."

With that he rose and went toward the door with Jesse behind him. Just before reaching the dugout he stopped short and cocked an ear toward the east. "I knew it. I knew it. I knew it," he said in a smug voice. "When you was talking about Tracey I thought I heard 'em. Now I sure as hell do. You was followed, my boy."

Jesse followed Harlan's lead and cocked his own ear eastward. "I don't hear anything," he said, "and I know I wasn't followed. Don't you think I had sense enough to check my back trail after the run-in I had with Cain?"

"Checked 'er or not, you was followed. And by a whole passel of them danged varmints, too. Why I bet they're strung out for dang nigh a quarter-mile."

"Okay. Okay," Jesse grinned knowingly. "What are you up to, you old devil. Just who followed me out here?"

Harlan carefully looked up and down the canyon before answering in a hand-covered whisper. "Ants."

Jesse had better sense than to respond.

"Sugar ants," Harlan said seriously. "Strung out for at least two hills behind you and nipping at yore butt like the Hounds of Hell after Hanna the Harlot."

All Jesse could do was grin as Harlan ducked his head to enter the dugout. Jesse followed him.

There would be no visiting with the new Mrs. Coldiron that night. She was lying on the single bunk, her feet still on the floor, sound asleep. Harlan smiled as he looked at her sleeping form, the dim candlelight flickering off her soft skin, the long braid pulled across her breast. He pulled off her boots, put her legs on the bunk while Jesse covered her with a tanned wolf pelt.

"Jesse," Harlan whispered, "I'm damned proud for the both of you. One thing you are is a man of your word, and if you say you'll take care of her, well then I know you will. And I can say that there's not a man alive that I'd rather leave my Tracey with than you. Do you think Cain will just let her go?"

"No."

They spread their blankets on the floor, put in more wood on top of the coals in the stove, adjusted the damper, and snuffed out the candle. With the moon now far below the rim of the canyon, the inside of the dugout was dark as pitch. After five minutes of absolute quiet Harlan whispered, "Jesse, you asleep?"

"Yeah."

"This is yore wedding night."

"Really?"

"Well, there's something about you an' Tracey an' the wedding that's still bothering me."

"What is it, Harlan?"

"It's sorter personal. But it's troubling me worse'n a case of the hiccups."

"What is it, Harlan?"

"Well, I was wondering about the celerbating, I mean you being married now an' all."

"Harlan, why in the thunder do you keep talking about celebrating? Celebrating what, for crying out loud? I couldn't be any happier about Tracey, that's for sure. But I haven't exactly been celebrating, not like you and me used to celebrate anyway."

Jesse heard the little man twist around in his blankets and whisper louder. "Coldiron, you know what's the matter with you? You're dense as a bucket of rocks, that's what. You might can write yore name and read it back, too, but if you ast me, you're on the verge of being plumb non-literatured. You run into some respectable words an' you're throwed before you can gather up the reins. Hell, I didn't say *celebrating,* I said *celerbating.* And I guess I'll have to explain it to ya. Celerbating is the act of avoiding any inanimate contact with women members of the other sex; to obstinate from the same folks. That's what celerbating is. Now, do you wanna talk about it?"

Jesse laughed a little. Then he laughed a lot. He tried to talk but couldn't. Finally, with intermissions for soft laughter, he managed to say, "Harlan, why don't you go water your lizard?"

CHAPTER
16

During the short hours that they slept, a stiff south-west wind had picked up, and it was that wind, rattling the slab door and the loose-fitting window just at the first faint crack of dawn on the fifth of December that awoke the sleeping occupants of the dugout. It was Tracey who awakened first, and she did so with a start.

What was that noise? That banging? Cain? She sat up in the middle of the bunk, but it was in no way familiar to her. Where *was* she? Her panicked mind could make no sense out of the strange place she was in, the rattling and banging, or the one small window in front of her through which could be seen the faintest of light. Flinging back the wolf-pelt cover, she bolted for that single square of faint light—but instead, collided with the table.

Jesse was on his feet in an instant, ready for action. "Tracey! What is it?" he said in a loud whisper on his way to the window, rifle in hand, fully dressed but barefoot.

Tracey calmed, sat back down on the bunk. "Oh . . . Jesse. It's nothing. . . . I woke up and couldn't remember where I was. I was scared. And then the noise."

Jesse struck a match and held it to the candle on the table. With the yellow flame highlighting the creases in his rugged face, he looked at her and started to speak, but before he could do so Harlan sat up on the floor where he had slept and said through a yawn, "By jiggers, it don't take long to spend the night around here anymore."

Jesse turned and looked at him. "Shoot, Harlan," he badgered with a grin, "look out that window there, we're already burning daylight. We shoulda done been across the river by this time a day."

And, in less than an hour, they *were* across the river; but it could hardly be said that they had burned much daylight, because even by then the sun could not be seen from the river bottom.

They made their way eastward, staying next to the river, using the profusion of cottonwoods and the salt-cedars for concealment. The weather was unusually warm and windy for December; they unbuttoned their coats, pulled their hats down tighter, and squinted their eyes against the stinging, wind-borne river sand.

For two twisting, choking miles, they dodged the thickest parts of the salt-cedar thickets, threw up arms to protect their faces against the lash of long, thin branches, and ducked their heads now and then so their hats would take the blows their arms missed.

Harlan, of course, was talking. He was telling Jesse all about salt-cedars and their absolute uselessness to anything that walked, crawled, or flew upon the face of the earth. Jesse could only catch about every fourth word but he grinned and nodded or frowned and shook his head at seemingly appropriate times. His gestures must have been synchronized with Harlan's talk because the old man seemed content with the responses he drew and he never slowed for anything other than an occasional dusty breath.

Jesse cared little for learning the merits or demerits of salt-cedars. All he cared about then was that they were concealing their advance on Loss Ess Canyon. His thoughts were on his bride of less than twelve hours, alone in the dugout. As is usually the case, it was circumstance that dictated what their course of action would be; Tracey had to stay by herself while Jesse and Harlan went to Loss Ess.

By the time they had found a trail, steep and rocky, that carried them to the flats and the hills above the river, their horses were sweated out like it was July. No longer was there a strong wind to catch the sweat and cool down their heated muscles; it stopped as they started up the trail just as suddenly as if someone had slammed a door shut cutting off the draft.

They stopped just after topping out above the river, let the horses catch their breath, tied their coats onto the backs of their saddles. They were three-quarters of a mile west of Loss Ess, separated from it only by a few rocky hills, scattered mesquites, cholla cactus, and dark green cedars. Harlan leaned on his horse's rump and looked toward the north. "Jesse," he said slowly, "I don't figure we oughta tie 'em on too tight, looky yonder."

Jesse was squatted down, rolling a cigarette. He stood, licked the paper and turned in the direction of Harlan's yonder. Interposed between the soft blue of the sky and the horizon he saw a much darker, ominous-looking blue. It was barely visible and he could see no clouds; just a suddenly darker sky above the horizon, and to those not familiar with Panhandle weather it might have gone unnoticed.

Jesse nodded, lit the cigarette. "Yeah," he drawled, "looks like the weather gods haven't been loafing all this time—they been brewing us up another norther."

The horses were hobbled in a cedar-filled saddle three hundred yards west of where two cowboys lay on their bellies on top of a big rock and underneath the spreading boughs of a wind-twisted rimrock cedar. Loss Ess Canyon was not particularly different from the many others that had formed during the last few hundred thousand years and that owed their existence to the Canadian River, which from time to time they fed with rampaging red water collected from hillsides and small streams during infrequent gully-washers. It was a little longer than most—some two miles from stem to stern—but not as long as some; a little deeper—some five hundred feet—than many, but not as wide as most that had obtained its length; it contained more springs than most, but not as much grass. While the canyon walls were not vertical, they were close enough to it that no horse or cow could negotiate either a climb up or a voyage down. The steep slopes sported big and little pieces of rimrock, scattered sagebrush, buffalo grass, and scrub cedars. There were places where there were none of these things, but instead an escarpment of lavender and gray and red, laced with fingers of clear gypsum.

Down in the canyon, many cattle were scattered along a wide, dry creek bed. Jesse knew some of the cattle were his and Harlan's without ever having to see brand-scarred hide or knife-marked ear. And, even from that vantage point, he could tell they had lost considerable flesh since last he had seen them some two weeks ago—but that was no surprise since they had traversed over a hundred miles of prairie and endured not one, but two snowstorms. It didn't require a very nimble mind to know that if they had to stay in that grazed-out canyon much longer they would be thin as a rail and in no shape for a return trip to Colorado.

Their gnarled-cedar observation post was about midway from where the canyon proper began and to where it opened into the river, but such was the curve of the gorge that neither end could be seen by them.

They pulled back from the rim for a quick parley. After a short discussion, they separated again, going in opposite directions along the canyon rim. During the next hour and a half of belly-crawls they saw the south end of the canyon, sixty feet wide and guarded by one man; and the mouth of the canyon, half a mile from wall to wall and necessitating three men to seal it off, either from escape of the cattle inside, or intrusion of uninvited guests from outside. They also saw many more cattle, some theirs and some not, but all, Jesse figured and Harlan concurred, as cheaply gotten as their own.

When they rejoined to pool their knowledge they could feel a north breeze and see that the thin layer of dark blue along the northern horizon earlier had trebled in thickness. White scudding clouds were forming in front of the ominous backdrop.

"Well, Mister Ramrod," Harlan said, "got any idees?"

"Just one that comes to mind right off," Jesse answered. "Let's go down there and tell them fellers that if they don't give us back our cattle we'll be obliged to shoot 'em in the head, much as we'd dislike having to do it."

"Uh huh, me and you being such crack shots and

all, and having such mean reputations as gunfighters, I guess it's done cut'n dried that they'll do 'er, too."

"Yeah, that's the way I got it figured. See any flaws?"

"No. That is, unless they notice that the cylinders on our shooting irons haven't been turned in so long they're rusted down solid, and about four generations of spiders have been reared in the barrels with all of 'em still living at home an' doing fine."

They decided maybe a revised plan should be submitted to the corporate board of Coldiron and Harrell Cattle Company. But what? That question drew only scratching in the dirt, a rubbing of chins, and the rolling of smokes in response. They both knew that the single guard at the south end of the canyon could be overpowered, but in riding up the narrow canyon to get the cattle everything would be boogered and sent to the mouth where the other guards were—thus getting back to the original plan and its original drawback, that being, the likelihood of those guards desiring to see certain rusty cylinders and certain cob-webbed gun barrels turn and smoke.

These two cowboys were just that—cowboys. And damned good ones, too. But gunfighters? No. They were decent shots with rifles for the simple reason that a rifle, with its longer sighting plane and steadier, against-the-shoulder shooting position was much easier to shoot accurately than a short-barreled handgun. A rifle did not demand as much instinctive shooting, and thus required less practice. A four-and-a-half-inch-barreled Colt, on the other hand, had been known to digest thousands and thousands of rounds every month for months on end before its owner became proficient enough to become deadly with it. Those thousands upon thousands of rounds had to be manufactured in the East, shipped west to a store owner—who had to realize a profit on them; so by the time all of that was summed up, the price tag on a 100-round box of 255-grain soft lead .45 caliber cartridges driven by 40 grains of FFg black powder read somewhere between two and three dollars per box; which meant that the average cowpuncher could hardly justify the cost of becoming an expert short-gun man. That is, if that cowpuncher intended to remain in that line of low-paying work.

It was a matter of priorities. As long as a man was a cowpuncher, his sidearm could be thought of as a utility tool, very useful for dispatching snakes and skunks, or for turning it around and using the butt to tighten a loose horseshoe or to knock the coffee grounds out of the bottom of the coffee pot, or for an occasional splurge at the end of a trail drive—or any other reason found to celebrate—when a man could get a little drunk and shoot it into the air a conservative time or two. After all, cowboys did have their rip-roaring image to uphold. An all-purpose tool, pure and simple.

But now, if that cowpuncher branched out into the cattle business or the banking business or the railroad business or the stage business, where the financial gains could be expected to be much greater, but also where the entry into them—and longevity in them—demanded that the former all-purpose tool become a well-oiled, precision instrument of life and death, then no expense would be considered too great for practice with and maintenance on that precious chunk of metal.

But Jesse and Harlan had been cowboys from the word go, and they fully intended to remain thus, albeit self-employed ones. So, the dirt-scratching and the chin-rubbing and the cigarette-smoking continued and the pleasant north breeze became more and more pleasant until, at length, the men gave up the scratching, rubbing, and smoking and proceeded to untie their coats from the backs of their saddles. It was while Jesse was tending to this task that his eyes fell on the thirty feet of hard-twisted, coiled, grass-fiber rope that hung back from the fork of his saddle. His brown eyes lingered upon it. A tanned hand left the saddle strings and gingerly, lovingly, touched it. When, at last, Jesse put on his coat and turned back to his partner, his countenance had undergone a change: His brown eyes sparkled, a wide grin exposed the chipped front tooth, and, had he been a cat, his mouth would have been flush with feathers.

Harlan took one look at his partner and forgot the increasing sting out of the north. "Coldiron," he said, "it 'pears to me that you've guessticulated something."

Jesse could not suppress the glee in his voice. "Partner," he said, "knowing how the Oldham County Commissioners, the Oldham County law, and the Panhandle Cattlemens' Association seem to have stacked the deck on us, how would you take it if they all of a sudden throwed in to help us get our cattle outa this canyon?"

"If," said Harlan seriously, "you said you really thought they would, then I'd take it you'd done gone bare-headed one too many times in the sun and that it's just now a catching up with you. That's how I'd take it."

Jesse would elaborate no more, but said they had to split up once again and watch each end of the canyon until the routine of the guarding duties had been ascertained.

The wind increased and the temperature was dropping. Harlan pulled up the collar on his coat. "It's going to be colder than a January baptizing just sitting on that rim," he grumbled, "but if we has to do 'er, then we'll do 'er. I just hope that this plan of yorn is better than the one you had about us breaking that cold-jawed horse from running off by you a-forefooting him whilst I was riding him. An' I hope it's a mite better than the idee you had about us throwing all them yankees outa the Bloated Goat Saloon in Kansas City by ourselves, all two, by God, dozen of 'em. And I hope it's better'n the one . . ." Jesse could still hear the old man mumbling as he disappeared down a steep incline on his way to the mouth of the canyon.

By the time they were positioned to watch for however long it took for an entire guard rotation to pass, the wind was blowing coattail-popping hard straight out of the north; and the temperature had dropped a good twenty-five degrees since they had first spotted the innocent-looking, dark-blue ridge in the north. Now, the leading edge of those clouds was past them and the only part of the once-bright sky that had not been violated by the fast-moving cloud mass was in the extreme south.

True to Harlan's prediction, it was damn cold just sitting or lying on top of the rimrock, being as still as possible and not daring to light a warming fire. Jesse snuggled himself into a growthy, rimrock cedar, while Harlan sought some protection from the wind by wiggling between two large rocks that contained a large, pyramidal pile of prairie-land waste deposited there by an industrious packrat. Behind the stack of dead prickly pear, dry bear-grass pods, small white bones, droppings of bobcats, coyotes, raccoons, deer, antelope, and parts of dried and broken cow chips, Harlan had a good view of the smoke bellowing up from the fire that was in front of a comfortable-looking wind-break. At this he sent numerous silent and vile oaths, growing less silent and more vile as time crawled by and the temperature continued to descend.

The hours passed and the only two nonindigenous mammals present along the entire length of that rim-rock remained motionless and frozen. A few flakes of powdery snow were angling toward the ground from the leaden sky. The two hobbled horses turned tail to the wind and grazed the hours away. By the time Jesse slid up next to Harlan, a thin veil of white covered the ground.

Once again they withdrew to collaborate. Harlan's reconnaissance report was: The guards in the mouth of the canyon were changed every three hours; a picket corral was located just inside a thick growth of trees toward the interior of the canyon a couple of hundred yards from the windbreak; a lone rider had arrived at the camp, stayed for an hour or so and then left again.

Jesse's report: His guards were also changed every three hours; they came and went by riding up and down the canyon; the guard on duty most of the time spent as much time stretched out in the grass—on the downwind side of a rock wall—napping as he did anything else; that and drink whiskey was about all he did the entire three hours. When he heard his relief coming he slid the bottle elbow-deep into a badger hole at the front of the rock wall.

"A man after my own heart," Harlan stated with a wide grin.

"Yeah," Jesse agreed, then added, "that's what I was counting on. Knowing you like I do I figure you're not far from a bottle right now."

Harlan flashed a big grin, walked joint-cold to his

horse, reached deep into his saddle bag and pulled out a pint of Old Crow.

They shared one drink before Harlan settled down out of the wind and offered the bottle to Jesse for a second. Jesse shook his head and said with a grin and to Harlan's consternation, "Better save the rest of it for that new guard on the south end. I think he's going to be cold enough to drink the whole bottle by himself."

CHAPTER 17

The guard at the south end—the beginning end—of Loss Ess Canyon was doing what most men do when they are bored and uncomfortable—he was examining his lot in life. At this particular cold time he was lamenting his involvement in a life of cattle stealing. He was not lamenting it because it was an unscrupulous and dastardly way to earn a living; but because there had been only one short swig left of what men of a certain rough nature relish on so cold a day as this one had become.

The man who employed the Loss Ess guards had made it clear enough that there would be no whiskey consumed until these cattle were driven out of the Panhandle. And, though these men believed themselves to be tough, none cared to match himself against J. W. Cain. So they did what all prudent men of like character would have done under similar circumstances —they drank in secret. They concealed their indulgence not only from Cain, but from one another as well. There was always the possibility that someone might tell Cain; but the main reason they drank in secret was the more alarming possibility that they might have to share their whiskey. So the guard at the south end of Loss Ess Canyon was understandably miserable over the empty whiskey bottle in his hand.

His fellows called him simply, Big Perce, due, no doubt, to his size and his unlikely given name of Percival. It was while Big Perce was silently listing the dozens of different places that he would rather be, or the many different things he would rather be doing, that he first heard the discordant refrain. He had no idea who was rendering the refrain nor where it came from, but this he did know—the singer was drunk and headed in his direction.

Big Perce, having his horse hobbled in a small growth of cedars, listened for a few more seconds and then joined his horse in the cedars.

In a matter of seconds, a sorrel horse carrying a rider rounded a bend in the creek. The horse was picking its own slow pace, at times coming to a complete halt before finally putting forth another forefoot and taking another step. The rider the sorrel carried was, as best as Big Perce could tell, an old-timer and small. With his turned-up coat collar touching his pulled-down hat, he reminded Big Perce for all the world of a drunk terrapin. This inebriated turtle swayed precariously in the saddle and sang as he rode the sorrel right up to the rock wall where Big Perce had been a few moments ago.

At such moments, time passes slowly. It seemed to Big Perce that the man must have died, or at least passed out in his saddle, for he sat there as still as any statue, and as silent, for an eternity—actually, but half a minute—before dismounting. Actually, it was more of a tumble. Once on his feet in the sandy creek bed, the old man continued his swaying and singing. Though unable to pick out a single pair of notes that belonged where the old man had put them, Big Perce did recognize the words as belonging to a ballad he had heard about a girl named Barbara Allen.

"In Longdun shi-i-ty, where ah onct did da-wa-hell," came the awful crooning that made Big Perce grin and decide to remain in the cedar and watch. The old sot knelt in front of a badger hole and began digging in that hole and throwing sand out of it and between his hind legs with such speed and dexterity that any badger of the long-furred, long-clawed variety would have been envious. It was too much for Big Perce. He stepped out of the cedars enjoying the best and most audible laugh he had known for some time. He laughed and the old drunk continued to dig and throw sand between his legs and sing and hum to himself in that way that only drunks can manage. Big Perce was beside himself with wild laughter, but the little man stayed with his digging and never once looked up or gave any indication that he knew he was no longer the only person in the creek bed. Finally, Big Perce tempered his humor, spat a long stream of tobacco juice into the sand, and said, "Hey, you ol' bastard, what'n the hell you doing?"

Harlan still gave no inkling that he had heard a thing; he went right ahead with his digging, throwing, and singing, "Ah courted 'er fer se'em long 'ears. . . ." He stopped abruptly, and Big Perce believed that the sound of another voice had finally registered and the old-timer would now turn around to see who was there; but instead, he lit into singing again, as far out of tune as ever: ". . . er maybeso it wuz ni-yun."

Now Big Perce stepped closer, to within an arm's length, but before he could speak again, the drunk below him stopped digging and said, "By gaud, ol' chawp, I do believe ya have suthin' there, ah do, ah truly do, sir." And with that he pulled forth the bottle that Jesse had promised would be in that particular hole. It was a quart of Jack Daniel's, half full, and the sight of it made Big Perce's eyes grow as large as the bottom of that round bottle. Harlan cradled the bottle close to his breast and patted it lovingly, still mumbling his love for "Bar'ra Al'n."

"Hey, you stupid ol' goat," said Big Perce, more shouting than talking, and only inches from Harlan's ear.

Harlan, lowering his tone and slowing his cadence, twisted around and looked over his shoulder into the ugly face of Big Perce; but instead of acting surprised, he leaned even closer, crossed, uncrossed and then recrossed his squinted eyes as if looking into the distance, then shrugged his shoulders and turned his attention to the cradled bottle again. With a twist of the wrist he jerked out the cork, inspected it at the tip of his nose with crossed eyes, licked it with his tongue, and then tossed it over his shoulder, hitting Big Perce under the left eye.

Holding the uncorked bottle in front of him, Harlan slurred, "I drink a toast to the ladies all." Then the bottle went up and Big Perce's eyes followed a large air bubble as it worked its way out of the slim neck of that bottle.

This time Big Perce got close enough to count the hairs in the old drunk's ear, and this time it *was* a shout. "You better git ta hell outa here!"

Harlan, pretending surprise, turned around without rising and said, "Fine, my good man, an' how are you? You want a little suthin' to ward off the cold?"

Big Perce looked at the bottle, licked his lips, looked

back at the old man, then back at the bottle. It was, of course, cut and dried what he would do next. "How long you had this stashed here?" he asked as he took the bottle. He turned it up, took a very healthy drink, wiped his mouth with the back of a gloved hand and handed it back to the old man, who said, "Ah dunno, fer ever an' ever ah reckon." Harlan patted the sand beside him. "Ah might fergit when ah hid suthin' but ah ne'er fergit where ah done it. Jist like a el-ee-fun't."

Big Perce didn't eyeball the half-full bottle of Jack Daniel's but a second before he became amicable enough to sit in the sand beside the old drunk. "What ta hell," he said, thoroughly convinced of the righteousness of his decision, "I'll have a couple of snorts, being's how it's so blamed cold and all. But then," he added, the amicable attitude waning, "you'll have to git on that horse an' sang an' stagger your way outa here jist like you sunged and staggered it in, you savvy?"

A twisted grin acknowledged Harlan's savvy, but Big Perce missed it because the uplifted Jack Daniel's bottle blocked his sight. After that second long drink, Big Perce looked at the bottle in his big hand and said, as he brought it to his lips again, "Hell, who's counting dranks, eh?"

Harlan took the bottle, lifted it to his lips, and handed it back to Big Perce, who partook of his fourth drink in stone silence. And so the fifth. Before the sixth drink reached his pursed lips the little man sitting beside him, the former "ol' bastard" and "stupid ol' goat" had been magically transformed into his "li'le friend" to whom he toasted the seventh drink.

Though the bottle had passed back and forth, Big Perce never noticed that each time it was delivered to him it was nearly as full as it had been when he handed it off. Or, if he noticed it, he was silently pleased and in no mood to mention the fact and take a chance on abating his good fortune.

By the time the eighth and ninth drinks had been consumed, the bottle was drained of its last drop, and Big Perce's eyes and his voice were all the worse for it. He said, "It's a totdamned good thang that bottle's empty 'cause if'n I drank much more I'd be startin' to git lit, an' that broad-butted bastard I work for said if anybody done that it'd be the last time for 'em to do it here, or anywheres else. An' ya know what, li'le friend, that sonabitch means 'er, too."

Harlan flashed the twisted grin at his well-oiled friend again, rose on wobbly legs, made his way, at last, to his sorrel, dug deep into his saddlebag and produced the pint of Old Crow that he and Jesse had each taken a drink out of an hour earlier. He staggered his way back to his sand-seat in front of the rock wall, pulled the cork out of the bottle and lifted the whiskey to his mouth. As he lowered the bottle, he looked at the cork in the same disgusted way he had inspected the first one and disposed of it in like manner. "Well," he mumbled, "we'll jist finish this'n 'fore ah go. Ta hell with all the broad-butted bosses in the whole broad-butted world, eh big man?"

The bottle was put right under Big Perce's nose but he showed much more will power than Harlan suspected him of possessing. "You don't know *my* goddamned boss," he declared. "I ain't drinking no more, an' that's that. Now you better git yore ol' butt outa here!"

Big Perce was a man well traveled, or at least so he thought. He had been to two South Texas goat ropings, one Mexican hanging, three county fairs, and any number of hog killings and cider drinkings—but, he had never, ever, heard of an old drunk pulling a gun on a man and telling him to drink the last of his whiskey. That was why he laughed when the old geezer beside him unlimbered his six-shooter and told him to get to drinking and not to stop. The laughter gave way to true bewilderment when the .45 came to full cock and was jabbed so hard under his nose that he could smell the Dupont black powder heating up.

Harlan let him catch his breath twice before the bottle was as empty as the first one; by which time Big Perce was face down in the snow-frosted sand of Loss Ess Creek, out cold.

Reholstering the .45, Harlan enjoyed a laugh. He did so with a mixture of humor and self-incrimination: The humor arose from the thought of Big Perce trying to convince his fellow guards that an old drunk came by, miles and miles from town, pulled a gun on him and made him drink so much he passed out; the self-incrimination came from the soul-rendering thought that if Jesse's plan failed to work, all of that good drinking whiskey would have gone for naught, in which case he could never forgive either himself or the Chairman of the Planning and Advising of Coldiron and Harrell.

Before Harlan had coaxed Big Perce into taking his third pull on the first bottle, Jesse was two miles south of them, among the hills and breaks that reached upwards from either side of the cold, dry, narrow creek. He was making a wide, fast, sweeping search for one thing—and by the time the second bottle had been opened, he found it—a small herd of cows, each clad in Longhorn hair and horns with an underbit earmark in each ear and an LS brand on each side. The particular herd that Jesse had jumped numbered about thirty head. They threw up their rangy heads and ran like deer when they saw him coming.

By the time Big Perce's left nostril was being introduced to Harlan's Colt, about half the herd had been held together and hazed—if an all-out, chap-slapping run could be called a haze—into the creek bed toward the head of the canyon.

By the time Harlan pulled Big Perce into the cedars along the creek, he could faintly hear the rattle of hoofs and horns, the sharp report of flying horses' hoofs on sandstone. Hurriedly, he pulled both cinches of his double-rigged saddle tight, mounted, and spurred in the direction of the pounding hoofs.

As he rounded the first bend in the creek, he saw the Longhorn cows running toward him with Jesse right behind them. He left the creek bed, circled around the small herd of cattle, and sided his partner.

Jesse looked at him, grinned wide and said, "Just like old times, eh?" His right hand went down, lifted the looped end of the rope-holding leather string from his saddle horn and pulled his rope free.

Coldiron's grin was returned by the little puncher now loping beside him. Harlan said, wild-eyed, "Hell, yeah, it'll be like ol' times if I shackle down two head whilst you're still chousing your first'n." The old hand already had his rope in hand and was busy shaking out a loop as he spoke.

They were in a long lope behind the cows, angling into the strong north wind, neckerchiefs and coattails flapping, eyes squinted against the stinging wind and the occasional snowflakes—but they were smiling and happy. This was their environment, their home, their domain. They would never outgrow the thrill of running headlong, hell-bent-for-leather, over rough terrain in hot pursuit of racing cattle, with big loops whirling overhead. Their horses, Jug and the sorrel, were not neophytes at this game; they knew what was about to take place and their adrenalin was pumping as fast as that rushing through the veins of the men on their backs; they were nervous now, chewing on the bits, ready for the chase to begin.

A mile upcreek from where Harlan and Big Perce had polished off the two jugs of hooch, a red-roan cow quit the bunch and left the creek on a southerly route, the wind pushing her on. "See ya, old man," Jesse yelled as he pulled down his hat and reined Jug in her direction.

The red-roan had already run three miles, but when she saw and heard the big brown horse knocking out her tracks she put her scrawny tail into a figure 9, lowered her horned head, and "left the flat" as fast as four churning legs has ever carried hide and horns. She made a wide turn, with Jug following her every wiggle but still two steps too far back for Jesse to throw; then she turned and headed into the wind. Over, around, and through cholla cactus, prickly pear, mesquite bushes, big rocks and little they flew; across dangerous badger holes, hidden gopher and sink holes they sped with no thought of checking; all of these things meant nothing, the chase everything. Jug's ears were laid back on his outstretched neck. Jesse was standing in his stirrups, leaning forward slightly, swinging a patient loop, while his spurs gently urged even greater speed from the brown mass of muscle under him.

They were almost back to the creek when Jug at last made up the two steps and put Jesse just where he wanted to be. Wanting more weight in his loop to counteract the wind, he loosened his grip on the rope and let a few more inches slide into the loop without ever slowing his swing.

The loop shot out. While ten inches of Colt revolver might have been but two and a half pounds of lifeless metal in those rough hands, thirty feet of catch rope became a predatory thing. Just as eagle talons gather in a fleeing prairie dog, so that darting circle of hemp gathered in a pair of upturned horns.

Jesse took the slack out of the loop with a jerk of the wrist and grinned as the cow snorted and slung her head in a vain effort to dislodge whatever it was that had pounced on her. Through the head-slinging and the snorting she never slowed her pace, nor did Jug slow his. The big gelding had been through the routine before, many times; he knew what Jesse was going to do next and was more than prepared when the slack was flipped over the cow's right hip. He summoned what reserve of strength he had, passed the cow on the left and then turned out, putting forth every bit of speed he had into his ground-hugging run, knowing that the harder he hit the end of the rope, the less jerk he would feel when the slack came out.

The rope between the nine hundred pounds of cow and the twelve hundred pounds of horse hummed tight and crackled—but it held. The cow's fore end swung around to the right, cleared the ground only an instant before her hind end followed; she hit the ground hard and flat with a sudden expulsion of air—from *both* ends—and with all four feet pointed in the same direction. Jug dragged her across the grass until Jesse was certain that she was down for good, or at least long enough for him to get down the rope and put a pair of rope shackles on her.

With the shackles on a front and hind foot, Jesse remounted and rode Jug toward the cow to take off the rope. The cow struggled and fought the shackles and bawled like something gone mad—and she was. Jug's sides heaved and his nostrils flared and closed in hard breathing. Jesse also breathed heavily; he pulled off his hat and wiped the sweat from his forehead with a coat sleeve, but he felt alive, felt good. His eyes swept the shadowless landscape until they picked out his partner, half a mile away—and just finished shackling a dun-colored cow. The old devil beat anything he had ever seen: Most of the time he acted as stove-up as a foundered horse, but when it came to shackling wild cattle he seemed to have a way of shedding thirty years.

Though Jug was still gasping for air, and Jesse was wondering why his coat had not been as effective when he was freezing to death on the canyon rim earlier, there wasn't time to rest or cool off. He and Harlan needed to shackle one more cow each, and the rest of those spooky cows weren't going to stand around like milk-pen calves and wait for them. He mounted again, touched his rowels to sweaty brown hair, and went after number two.

Before many more minutes had passed the chore was done, and four disgruntled LS cows were "blowin' snot" into the sand, all within sight of each other, all as determined as the first one had been to break free and none having any more success than she in doing so.

The cowboys next checked on the drunken guard, built up his small warming fire—that was about to be the branding fire—and let the horses get a well-earned breather. After that, they spent an hour in double-horse leading each cow to the head of the canyon where the guard was dozing, and the branding fire was heating a cinch-ring running iron.

Carefully—both men were well aware of the consequences if an LS man should happen along—the cows were branded. Two of them, the red-roan and the dun, were branded in such a way that the LS was changed into a 48. Since the LS outfit branded on both sides, one side had to be branded, the cow rolled over and branded again.

"I reckon," mumbled Harlan, squinting in the acrid branding smoke, "that them LS boys ain't figured out that where one side of the critter goes, the other'n usually tags along."

A young red-and-white spotted cow with small horns had the L in her brand changed into a 4, but the S was not changed in any way.

The last cow, an old Jersey-cross-looking thing, was hair-branded with the 48, but the hide itself was not burned.

After the last cow was branded, they were all released and turned into the canyon to mix with the cows already there. The tracks where the branding took place were rubbed out, as were all telltale tracks where the roping occurred. Big Perce was retrieved from the cedars and stretched out in front of the rock wall where he and Harlan had passed the bottle. The empty bottles were coldheartedly placed beside him.

With all of that done, there was but one thing left to do—wait up on the canyon rim until the next man came to relieve Big Perce so they could be sure the fresh-branded cows did not decide to leave before a more attentive guard came on duty.

Three miles west of Tascosa on a small ranch and among the many cottonwoods that lined Cheyenne Creek another man waited. But where the two cowboys waited in the cold of the dying day, this man waited in the warmth, amid the trappings and shipped-in Eastern finery of an eight-room adobe ranch house. And where the cowboys waited with a certain amount of satisfaction, this man did not. But he was not waiting alone; he waited with two old and dear friends—Hatred and Vengeance. They would have come calling this day at any rate after the occurrence at the North Star Cafe the night before, but with the early morning town talk of a certain wedding following that occurrence, they arrived hastily and were determined not to depart until *something* had been done. A third companion, Humiliation, had arrived belatedly but had failed to gain admittance. Each time Humiliation thought he would succeed in joining that circle of friends, he would be forcibly removed from the porch, tossed halfway to the barn and told by the host, J. W. Cain, never to show his face at the ranch again.

So now, J. W. Cain and his two malevolent friends waited. Exactly what it was they waited for they did not know, except that for the moment they waited for the Mexican cleaning woman to finish with the kitchen, where they were gathered. Cain looked at her as she stooped over to sweep sand into her dustpan. To take his mind off the repulsion and the contempt that swept over him at the sight of her, he looked out the window and watched the dry sand blow along the edge of the creek. He thumped on the oak table and gazed out the window.

"Adios, Señor Cain," the old woman said from the doorway as she struggled to get into her frayed coat, unaware of Hatred and Vengeance sitting at the table with him.

Cain offered her a small head-bob in return, unaccompanied by either word or smile. He watched her

184

shuffle out into the gray cold and the light snow. Before she reached the barn where her wagon and mule were, Slim came riding around the corner of the barn, dismounted in front of the house, clomped across the porch, and pushed open the door. He was smiling.

"You an' that old señorita have a good day, boss?" he jested.

Cain watched her lead the mule out of the barn and painfully climb into the wagon. "It'll be a cold day in hell before J. W. Cain has to rub up against something like that."

Deciding that it might be a wise move to change the subject, Slim turned to work. "It's starting to snow more out there. We still going t'morrow?"

"If the snow's less than belly deep we are. You told the men in Tucalo Canyon to be ready like I said, didn't you?"

"Yeah, they'll be ready to throw in with the rest of us when we get the other bunch there."

Cain nodded approval and, after a time in which his mind seemed to stray from the matter at hand, said, "I told the men in Loss Ess to have theirs bunched up by sunup and ready to go."

After a lengthy silence Slim asked his boss, reading his mind, "You see anything of them today?"

"No." Cain replied. Another lengthy silence followed until Hatred could stand it no longer: "A goddamned common cowhand! I can buy and sell 'em all day long for two bits. I bet if he had to come up with more than twenty-five dollars cash he'd have to hock his goddamn boots and hat."

Slim did not say anything.

Vengeance would not be outdone. "I got a feeling," said Cain, "that Coldiron doesn't have enough sense to leave the country and forget about his stupid cows. And I got another feeling that I'll see them both again real soon, and when I do Coldiron will be in hell and Tracey will wish she was. That's what I get for being nice to that little slut and letting her take her time. Well, J. W. Cain is through being nice.''

It was colder than ever and still snowing lightly, but the wind had quieted by the time the two weary but smiling punchers trotted west from the canyon rim and rode toward the big orange sun, barely visible in a small hiatus between the horizon and the gray clouds. Long shadows followed as they pointed their horses toward a little dugout whose day was already finished, the brief sun having fallen below the rim of Minneosa Canyon a half hour earlier.

CHAPTER
18

On the plains it is not unusual for darkness to descend slowly, for twilight to linger behind for an hour after the sun has set, for that twilight to give way in such a discreet and unheralded fashion to night that the transformation may be complete for some time before it is noticed. But not so this evening. With the heavy overcast the twilight had retreated with the sun, leaving nothing but a skim of dry snow to soften night's fall.

The swift arrival of such a black night caught even the two cowboys crossing the river by surprise. As they headed up Minneosa Canyon a sudden urgency gripped Jesse, and even though it was impossible to see the ground underneath their horses he cued Jug into a trot that was just short of a lope, and it was not until they rounded the last bend in the creek and saw a small yellow light a mile ahead and smelled the reassuring aroma of mesquite smoke and freshly boiled coffee that the unexplained tightness in his throat eased. Still, he did not slow to a saner gait nor relax in the saddle until he saw a slender figure silhouetted in the doorway.

Tracey watched as they pulled the saddles from the steaming backs of their horses and turned them loose to join her paint and the dun packhorse. The newest additions to the corral nosed the ground and wallowed while Harlan tossed them their ration of mesquite beans and Jesse carried an armful of wood into the dugout.

So great was the change in temperature from outside to in, that the men's ears tingled and their fingers became so stiff that rolling a cigarette was a slow, awkward chore. They sat at the crude table lit by a pair of candles, smoked Bull Durham and sipped steaming coffee poured by a smiling and vibrant Tracey. Her hair was pulled back from her face and plaited into one long braid that reached to the middle of her back. They needed no further convincing that there was no better place to be on a dark and cold night. The dugout was filled to capacity with warmth from the heart and from the cast-iron stove, soft flickering candle light, the smell of cooking supper, and lively talk about the day's events. Never had the little domicile known such congeniality, nor such a feminine touch, nor had any of the three known such a feeling of belonging.

An hour later, when the coffee pot contained more grounds than liquid, Harlan pushed back an empty plate and announced, "Time for me to hit the trail; I've got a lot of miles to cover."

Tracey was surprised. "You're going tonight?"

"Got to," Harlan answered as he slipped into his coat, "if I'm going to see Mr. W. M. D. Lee his humble self and convince him that there's some strange goings-on around Loss Ess that ain't exactly according to old Hoyle, like the sound of bawling cattle and the smell of singed hair where there shouldn't be none. And then getting back to Loss Ess by sunup tomorrow.''

When they were outside again Jesse started to speak but was cut off by Harlan's upraised hand. "Now Jesse," he said with an air of authority, "there ain't no use in us talking no more about it—I'm a-going and you're a-staying. You may be a good hand at a few things, but when it comes to talking you're worth about as much as a setting of rotten eggs. And this here deal calls for some mighty high-powered gum-bumping. You said so yourself.''

Jesse had to concede that fact.

"Besides that, old Lee'll come a danged sight nearer believing a man that's been trapping his country for two years than a man they just let out of jail.''

Jesse had to concede that fact, too.

"And," Harlan said, leaning toward the taller man before speaking lowly to him, "I reckon a man that's took a wife oughta stay with her.''

That third fact would have to be conceded as readily as facts one and two. But unlike the first two facts this third one was becoming more and more perplexing the closer Harlan got to leaving. The first two could be forgotten for now, but number three would have to be dealt with soon.

"Be damn careful," Jesse warned as his partner swung upon the back of the sorrel. "I'll see ya in the morning if everything works like it's supposed to. I just hope that Garrett is somewhere close, because I don't figure it'll do us much good if Lee has to send out some of his cowhands to see what'n the hell's going on. And I'll just bet anything that Cain's fixing to get them cattle outa here pretty pronto.''

Harlan nodded his agreement. "Yeah," he said, "see ya." And with that he disappeared in an instant into the blackness of the night and the increasing snowfall, leaving Jesse, and Tracey, alone to deal with fact number three.

It wasn't that Jesse's feelings for Tracey had changed since the night before; if anything he loved her even more. But what had happened in the grass beside the river hadn't been a planned thing any more than the fight with Cain had been. They had come together in a sudden rush, their passions not giving them time to think about what they were doing. But now, now that they were married, now that they would be alone with no one near and no hurry to get somewhere, it was different. And the difference was great enough that the same man who had a few hours ago handled twelve hundred pounds of horse and two nine-hundred-pound cows with finesse and ease was suddenly put very ill at ease by a hundred and fifteen pounds of young woman. He had never been to bed with a woman who was not on a schedule, with a woman he loved and who returned that love. Thus, as much as he loved the raven-haired beauty inside the dugout, as much as he wanted to make her happy, as much as he wanted to hold her and kiss her, he was reluctant to go back inside.

When he did return, Tracey immediately detected the change in him and feared that she had done something wrong. Maybe, she thought, he was having second thoughts about the sudden wedding. Or maybe, and this was her greatest fear and one that had not left her all day, he could not get the picture of her former life out of his mind. She loved Jesse Coldiron, her husband, more than she loved even life itself and wanted him to come to her and hold her more than she wanted to fill her lungs with mesquite-warmed air, but he was distant now, and cold.

So, with no forewarning, the amenity, the easiness, the relaxed atmosphere that had been in the dugout during supper had disappeared. Somehow, it had slipped out while Jesse was making last-minute plans with his partner. Where it had gone and why, neither was certain. Last night, in the North Star during supper, on the river bank, in Scotty Wilson's house, riding across the prairie, the talk had come as easy as a pebble scooting across pond ice. But now, alone in a small, dimly lit dugout with a full dark night in front of them, the few words came hard and forced, like they were having to be sledged through a too-small opening and were coming through the ordeal in odd, misshapen forms that neither recognized.

Jesse drank a last cup of coffee in tortured silence while Tracey finished washing the cooking and eating utensils, after which she sat on the dirt floor in front of the stove and began unbraiding her hair. Jesse couldn't keep his eyes off her, and yet he avoided her eyes, just as she avoided his, as if they were doors left open by chance and to look into them might catch the other in an embarrassing, private moment.

She had finished unbraiding her long, shiny hair and was starting to comb it out when Jesse pushed back from the table and stood. "I reckon I'd better check the horses," he said flatly. "I'll have to be leaving before daylight in the morning."

When he reached the door Tracey's soft voice reached him. "Will you be long?"

He turned back toward the voice and for the first time since Harlan left he looked into Tracey's eyes. "No," he said, "not long." He hesitated a moment and then went outside.

He checked to see that the gate to the corral was secure and threw plenty of dry hay over the fence. Snow was coming down harder and the flakes were bigger, but there was no wind to drift them—just big fluffy flakes falling out of a black sky and taking their own time about coming to earth. Jesse shaved and bathed in the cold spring as best as he could, got back in his clothes, and rolled a cigarette.

The door moved, then it stopped, then it opened like a sleepy eye that is not sure it is ready for the light.

Jesse stood in the doorway fresh shaven, dark mustache ending at the edges of his mouth and trimmed even with his upper lip, thinning brown hair combed and frosted with snow.

He was spellbound. In all of his life he had seen nothing to compare with the sight that his eyes looked upon now. He knew no artist, no matter how gifted his hand or dedicated his brush could ever come close to matching the beauty inside the dugout.

Tracey had snuffed out the candles, and the only light in the room was that coming from the open door of the cast-iron stove. She stood on a tanned wolf pelt in front of the stove, facing Jesse. Around her waist was another pelt, open on one side and showing a slim, smooth leg from foot to hip. Above her small waist nothing hid her beauty, nothing covered her but the soft flickering yellow light of slow-burning mesquite. Thick black hair fell over each shoulder and veiled the warm flesh of her breasts.

She looked at Jesse without embarrassment. "I thought you would never come," she whispered.

No one needed to tell them that love and contentment had returned just as suddenly as they had vanished. They kissed long, reveling in the taste of each other. His hard hands caressed the full length of her bare back, from the neck that was buried in sweet-smelling hair to the gentle curve of slim hips. The fire and the passion they had felt on the grass by the river was there, but now there was no frenzied hurry, no raging inferno that consumes everything and suddenly dies. The time was right. The night belonged to them.

Outside there was no sound, no movement. The horses were bedded down on the uneaten hay, asleep. The covey of blue quail underneath a low-spreading cedar were pressed close to one another for warmth, their feathers fluffed out to cast off any brush-intruding snowflakes. Even the spotted-bellied bobcat stuck his furry head out of his den, measured the night and decided it too dark, too cold, and too wet for good hunting, decided his warm, dry bed was more to his liking this night. The only movement was the slowly descending snowflakes. The only sound was the snuggling of one snowflake into another, as peaceful and quiet as two lovers on a soft wolf pelt in front of a shy, waning fire.

CHAPTER 19

And so passed the cold, dark snowy night of December fifth, 1884. It is enough to say that Jesse and Tracey's marriage was consummated, their commitment deepened, the sanctity of their union—both of body and of soul—even more heartfelt.

During that night the clouds embarked on an easterly course, leaving in their wake a dawn that was still, magnificently clear, and toe-numbing cold. The Panhandle had experienced an unusual occurrence—snow that had been allowed to remain just where it had fallen, snow unaccompanied by strong winds. A soft three-inch blanket of snow balanced precariously on cedar boughs, covered the grass and the rocks, and crunched under Jug's hard hoofs as he approached the rim of Loss Ess Canyon; crunched under the hoofs of two horses coming to the canyon from the opposite direction; crunched under the hoofs of five other horses not far behind those two.

The sun was slow in rising. It tinted the east, doused a few stars, and then seemed to stop in its tracks. It lay beneath the southeastern cover of snow for an eternity, only teasing warmth to the Panhandle.

Jesse was on the rim just above the canyon's mouth. Below him the cattle had been pushed into a milling herd. Five mounted men surrounded them in cold silence. Two more, just arriving, were between the herd and the river.

As he had feared, the cattle were being moved this morning. His eyes jumped the canyon and searched the opposite rim and the stretching plain beyond for his partner. No movement, no bobbing dark forms could be seen there. He looked down the river; the mile of it that he could see before a sharp bend cut his vision offered no more help than did the lifeless, rocky, snow-covered country above.

He backed away from the rim, rolled a smoke, and tried to stomp some warmth into his feet. As he flicked the cigarette butt into the snow he heard the "Yaws!" and the "Hey-Heys!" and the other usual yells and sounds that men use to get a herd of cattle moving.

He knew the time for waiting had passed. He mounted and loped to the trail that fell off the rim and descended to the riverbed flat below. He would intercept the herd and stop it. After that, he didn't know; he would just have to play each card as it fell. From the top of the rim he could see the herd clearly; he estimated its head count at about two hundred—big enough that the four fresh-branded cows hadn't yet been seen. Once the herd was strung out they would be spotted, and his plan would go the way the snow would go by late afternoon—down the river.

Once Jug was started down the trail he was given his head and Jesse reared back in the saddle for the rocky, snow-covered descent. They were midway to river level when two welcome and warming sights came to his eyes. The sight that warmed—or soon would—his toes and ears was a big orange sun just making its appearance over the horizon. The other sight warmed his heart—riders coming around the bend in the river.

While Jesse was admiring the countryside, Jug was having his problems getting them to the bottom of the slick trail in the same arrangement they had known when they started down, that is, with the man on top and the horse on bottom doing all the work. In his sliding and flouncing, he dislodged a saddle-blanket-sized flat rock and sent it downhill, taking several smaller companions with it and creating, by the time it reached the bottom, a mini-avalanche of rock and snow.

All seven of the men around the moving herd caught the sound at the same time. Cain and Slim were on point, and they stopped the herd and watched as the horse finished his descent and trotted toward them. At three hundred yards they recognized Coldiron, exchanged words, and widened the distance between them to twenty feet. Slim pulled his rifle out of its scabbard. Cain hardened his gaze and unbuttoned his coat.

When Jesse had closed to within a hundred yards of them he heard Slim work the lever of the rifle and make a remark about some cowboy's mental faculties that brought an agreeing sneer to Cain's lips. That sneer was still growing and never had time to reach its true potential because Slim saw the five riders coming at them from the other direction and said, "Goddamn, look there. You know who that looks like?"

J. W. Cain not only knew who it looked like, he

knew who it was. Once a man had seen Pat Garrett, he was not apt to ever mistake him for anyone else. His six-foot-five-inch frame stuck up a head taller than anyone else's; and when he was mounted his long legs hung so close to the ground that it was almost comical, especially so if he was riding a short horse.

The horse that carried Pat Garrett that morning would have been hard-pressed to measure more than fifteen hands, but the men coming out of the Loss Ess Canyon driving a herd of bargain-price cattle were not laughing. For the most part, they appeared as if they could have undergone ear-to-ear tonsillectomies and not have spilt a drop of blood. Jesse, pulling to a satisfied stop twenty feet in front of Cain, was smiling. Harlan Harrell, flanking Garrett, was smiling. And even the county sheriff was wearing what could have been described as a faint smile.

The five river riders stopped a few feet from the point of the herd where J. W. Cain, Slim, and Jesse Coldiron waited. Cain looked anvil-hard at Jesse, nurturing his sneer, before turning toward Garrett. "Hello, Garrett," he said, as cordially as possible, "what's the law doing out on a cold morning like this?"

Pat Garrett's detractors said that he squeezed every bit of gold and glory out of his much-ballyhooed shooting of Henry McCarty—alias William Bonney, alias Billy the Kid—that he could, and that he was not as brave a lawman and gunfighter as he wanted people to believe. After all, they said, it was a dark-room ambush and not a face-to-face shootout that had cost the buck-toothed killer his life. Some might argue over, Garrett's real role as a lawman, but no one could deny that he was an impressive figure, and a bad hombre to have down on you.

Garrett slowly surveyed the circumstances. His piercing blue eyes took in the herd of cattle, the men around it, Cain, Slim, and Jesse before saying, "What've you got here, Cain?"

"A handful of strays," Cain said, unflustered. "We were just fixing to drive 'em to Tascosa," he lied. "What brings you out this way?"

Garrett rested both big hands on the saddle horn before answering. "I got word last night that we might find some LS cattle here that'd had their brands changed. Know anything about it?"

"No," Cain said flatly, confidently, "not a thing."

Garrett leaned his lanky frame to the side, spat a long stream of brown tobacco juice into the snow and said, "This report allowed as how these LS cattle might be throwed in with a herd of strays and cattle wearing some of the outlawed brands."

With that summary the head of the Home Rangers looked at the cowboy on the big brown gelding, the one with the pleased look, the one that was in the county jail a few days ago. Finally, he said, "Coldiron, what do you know about this?"

Jesse, basking in the scorch of Cain's eyes, replied, "Oh, I don't know nothing about that. I was just out here enjoying the morning when I saw these fellers down here and just come down to chew the fat with 'em."

Garrett gave Jesse a go-to-hell look and then turned back to Cain. "I guess it'll be okay by you for us to look through these cattle."

Cain twisted around in his saddle, looked at the herd, tensed a little and said, "Go ahead. You won't find anything though."

* * *

Everybody—Jesse and Harlan, Jim East and the two rangers who came with Garrett included—scattered around the herd to help hold it while the tall man on the little horse rode through it, looking. Harlan recognized Big Perce, who had been twisting and squirming in his saddle like he had a live coal in his underwear all the while the talk had been going on, and, out of sheer orneriness rode all the way round the herd to be next to him.

"Howdy," Harlan said to the big guy, "mighty cold, ain't it. Yes sir, I kid you not, this here is dranking weather, ain't it."

For all the response his friendly overture brought him, Harlan might just as well have been talking to the horse underneath the big fellow next to him as to the fellow himself. Big Perce sat his horse as still as if he had been cast in bronze; the only giveaway that he was not was a nonmetallic oath coming from between his clenched teeth.

Garrett hadn't been in the herd long enough for a man to smoke one cigarette when he motioned for Cain and Jim East to come there. When they sided him, he pointed to a cow. And then another. Jesse caught Jim East's smile, Garrett's hard look at Cain. The look on Cain's face was a study in perplexity: The only look that Jesse could compare it to was that of a bait-stealing coyote that had just felt the pan of a number four Newhouse trap give way under his paw.

The three men in the herd looked at another cow, long and hard, and discussed her for some time. Finally, Garrett shook his head and said something to East who, in return, pulled his rope loose from the fork of his saddle, put one end of it over his saddle horn and built a loop in the other. The sheriff eased through the herd following the cow they had been discussing. When he was in the proper position he brought the big loop up smoothly over his head, turned it over, and flicked a perfect hoolihand with a swift motion of the wrist. The loop sailed flat and open and settled over the cow's head.

When East pulled the slack out of the loop, the cow went to the end of the rope, bawling and struggling. She was led, with proper application of cold steel to horse ribs, to the edge of the herd, where East motioned to Jesse with a nod of the head. Jesse knew in an instant what the nod meant and was shaking out a heel loop as he rode to the cow. He spurred Jug in behind her and threw his loop, picked up only one leg, turned the rope loose without taking out the slack and let the single leg go free. The next loop went around both hocks. This time, Jesse quickly pulled out the slack, snugged the rope around her legs, wheeled Jug around and put him into leaning against the rope. With the stout brown putting his weight against her on one end and Jim East's horse doing the same on the opposite end, there wasn't anything for her to do but bawl and fight her head and be stretched out in the snow.

Pat Garrett dismounted, walked to the side of the cow, pulled his right glove off, and rubbed the brand on her side—leaning over and getting his face to within a few inches of it in the process. After a brief, but expert and thorough, inspection, he raised his frame, looked at Jim East and announced, "That forty-eight's hair-branded over the LS, just like we thought. I don't reckon we need to check them other cows wearing a fresh brand."

With that remark, Garrett slipped his glove back on, grabbed the rope on the cow's head and pulled it off when East gave him slack. When the tall lawman had remounted, Jesse gave slack in the rope on his end and let the cow kick free.

Cain had been sitting quietly on his horse nearby all the time the inspection had been taking place, his face darkening with rage. As he watched the cow they had just released trot high-headed and mad back into the herd, Garrett came beside him and said in an even tone, "What've you got to say about this, Cain?"

J. W. Cain didn't say anything. His big jaw muscles bulged and his lowered eyebrows pointed menacingly toward the pleased-looking cowboy on the big brown horse. Finally, he smoothed his eyebrows and shifted his gaze back to Garrett. "Do you think I'd be stupid enough to do something like that?" he asked with a tone of indignation. "Hell, Coldiron's done it! Why do you think he's out here to start with? You didn't believe that crap of his about just being out here for a ride, did you?"

"No," Garrett said in the same even tone, "but it wasn't Coldiron and a bunch of his men driving the herd outa Loss Ess. I don't know what in the hell's going on here, Cain, but that whole damn herd's made up of strays, outlawed brands, and changed LS brands and there ain't none of 'em wearing your brand." After a short silence, spent in decision making, Garrett continued, "I think we'll just take these cattle, the whole herd, back to Tascosa with us. I want to see you there, too."

Jesse, nearby and trying to hide his grin, pretended to wipe a drip from his nose with the back of his glove.

"Coldiron," Cain said, slow and deep-throated and followed by a threatening silence that was broken by the remainder of the vow, "I'll see you in hell."

Jesse, still wearing a trace of the grin, said, "More'n

likely you will. You don't need to wait for me though, Mr. Cain. You get a chance to go any time soon, you go ahead. It'd be a dirty shame to turn the trip down just because I wasn't quite finished here.''

Cain pulled his coattail away from the butt of his six-gun. "I'll promise you one goddamn thing, Coldiron," he said mockingly, "you'll be an old hand down there while I'm still up here crawling into bed with a black-headed whore.''

Jesse's grin vanished in a flash, and his hand dropped toward his Colt.

Cain's .45 cleared leather, was on the way up smelling blood when Garrett spurred his horse between the two men. "Cain!" he ordered, "you ease that thing back into your holster! Coldiron! Back off!''

Death was hovering, waiting. The morning became suddenly very cold and quiet.

The metallic sounds of a .44–40 cartridge being driven into Jim East's rifle chamber twenty feet away could have been heard halfway to Tascosa, so loud and crisp-sounding was the action of his Winchester in the early-morning stillness. Jesse—whose weapon had never cleared its holster—let his gun drop the two inches it had risen. Cain, with the sneer returning to his face in full-blown conceit, lowered the heavy hammer of his Colt. He had measured Jesse Coldiron and found him wanting in every rule whereby he judged manhood: too short, too light, too weak, and much, much too slow and awkward with a gun. To kill the cowhand would be no more of a chore for him than killing a rattlesnake. It was, though, a chore that he had put off as long as he could stand; but one that would have to wait a short while yet.

"Now we know, don't we, Coldiron," he said. Then, shifting his gaze to Pat Garrett and tending to business at hand, he said only a little less hostile, "You haven't got any reason to be arresting me, Garrett."

"Never said I was," Garrett said. "I just said we're going to take the cattle back to town. But I do want you to come by the sheriff's office in a day or so and talk to me."

Cain was silent for a moment, then smiling on the surface but raging within, he said, "Sure, why not. Take the cattle. Like I said, we were headed to town with 'em anyway."

The sun had been up less than an hour, hadn't even started to loosen the snow's grip on the Panhandle, when J. W. Cain and his men sat in the mouth of Loss Ess Canyon and watched the cattle they had been guarding for days go down the river.

They sat thus for a long time while the boss cut off a chew of tobacco from a plug of Henry Clay, chewed it fiercely for a few minutes, spat three times into the snow, and kept his eyes riveted on the receding herd until it at last disappeared around the first river bend.

When their boss broke the silence they were surprised by how controlled and how confident his voice was in spite of suffering such a humiliating comeuppance. "Slim," he instructed, "you and Harry follow them, stay on top of the rimrocks and behind them always so they don't see you. If either Coldiron or old man Harrell head back this way pretty soon, come right back here; we'll wait for a couple of hours before going on to Tucalo Canyon. Slim, your job is to stay with the herd as long as either of 'em are with it. I got a hunch the old man will head back before long. If he does, Slim," here Cain took his eyes off the spot where the herd had disappeared for the first time since he broke his silence and put them on the man he was instructing, "you don't let that goddamn Coldiron out of your sight. If he heads back this way kill him, any way you want. Because if he gets to Tucalo and pulls the same thing, Slim, I'll kill you and then I'll kill him."

Harry and Slim left and those remaining dismounted to wait in a thick growth of trees. Before the allotted two hours was half consumed, Harry came loping back and greeted them with this affirmation: "You was right, Mr. Cain, the old man turned back upriver. You all woulda seen him go by here if them trees hadn't been in the way. He ain't much more'n a half-mile up the river by now. Slim, he kept on following Coldiron an' the cattle.

J. W. Cain grinned big, spit an extra load of tobacco juice an extra long distance and said, "Well now, it looks like old J. W. is finally getting a break. It just goes to show ya boys that if you just stay hooked long enough some good things will start happening. . . . and if that old man is headed where I think he is—well then, a thing that started off bad five years ago is going to wind up good. I mean"—here he paused and when he spoke again it was almost a whisper, pronounced through set teeth—"real goddamn good. Coldiron can have the cattle; I'd trade the stupid bastard ten thousand head for . . . Let's go boys. I think we're going calling."

CHAPTER 20

Every few seconds all morning long Tracey had looked out the single small window of the dugout. The thing her eyes scoured each and every time was snow-covered Minneosa Creek, looking like a twisting white road, growing smaller and smaller as it receded toward the place where it made a sweeping turn, touched the canyon's eastern wall, and then disappeared a mile south of the dugout. All morning long nothing—save for three mule deer—had ventured upon that ribbon of white. All morning long she had been nervously awaiting Harlan's return. All morning long, since the sun first climbed over the canyon's rocky eastern rim, she had been expecting to see him come around that wide turn of the creek. Before Jesse left, he had saddled her paint and packed the dun with everything they intended to take. But where was Harlan? Shouldn't he have been here long ago? Had something gone wrong? One short night in the arms of the only man she had ever loved, would ever love, was not enough. What they had found—by chance, by fate, or by whatever—was too good to risk losing because of a few cows. She had tried to convince Jesse of that fact as he saddled in the early-morning darkness, but her words had not changed his mind.

"Tracey," he had told her as he swung the saddle up, "those heifers are a lot more important to us than they ever were to me alone. They're a start, a chance." Then he had pulled the latigo tight and turned to face her, putting his hands on her shoulders. "But it ain't just the cattle, Tracey. Cain's got something that belongs to us, something that he took from us because he's big and strong and mean and knows how to take advantage of the law. Yeah, I suppose we could cut and run and survive without those heifers. Just like Juan Castillio decided to cut and run without his few cows after his brother was killed. But what about next time, and the next, and the one after that; 'cause there's always going to be somebody taking from the people he thinks won't, or can't, do anything about it. A man either stays and fights everytime or he cuts 'n runs everytime, 'cause whichever he does once, he's bound to do it again and again. And before long all he's doing is runnin'."

Tracey knew he was right. She even knew that's what he would say; that was one reason she loved him so. And yet, had it been her decision, they would have run. As fast and as far from J. W. Cain as they could. She feared that no one, Jesse and Harlan included, knew fully what the man was capable of.

Snapping her out of these thoughts was the realization that the horses in the corral were looking, with raised heads and forward-thrust ears, down the canyon. But though she tried desperately to see what it was that had their attention, all she could see was an empty, white wilderness. One of the horses in the corral nickered, head held higher, but still she could see nothing moving.

Then, there! There in the creek, coming around the wide bend. A rider! She watched the rider, framed in the window, lope up the creek and then watched him slow to a trot. She could see the horse's frosty breath as his lungs expelled short, rapid bursts of hard-riding hot air into the cold morning. She stood motionless in the dugout, studying the rider, more nervous now than when she could see no one. When, at last, she was sure that it was Harlan she heaved a sigh of relief and started for the corral.

She was mounted, holding the lead-rope on the dun's halter, when Harlan came beside her. Instead of greeting her in his accustomed smiling, talkative manner, and without giving her time to say how relieved she was to see him, Harlan took the dun's lead-rope from her and hurriedly said, "We gotta ride, Tracey! I spotted callers coming, not much more'n a mile behind." Tracey didn't reply, just dug her heels into the ribs of the paint, following Harlan's lead.

They were in the creek bed in an instant, headed north, up-canyon. But not fast enough; the dun was balky, would only stick out his head and trot no matter how hard he was pulled. Without a lost moment, Harlan handed the lead-rope back to Tracey, swung in behind the dun, took his rope from his saddle fork, and made rump dust and dun hair fly. The packhorse, deciding that the sting of the doubled rope was much more persuasive than cussing, put his head beside Tracey's left stirrup and loped on a loose rope all the way to the beginning of the trail that would take them out of the canyon and onto the open country above.

The trail was too steep, too snow-covered slippery for any gait other than a slow one. As their ascent was begun, Harlan silently cussed the virgin snow—without it recording their tracks, the men behind them would have to guess which way they had gone once they reached the grassy plain above.

By the time they were midway between canyon floor and rim Harlan knew he had overestimated the lead they had on their pursuers. A short half mile down-canyon and closing fast were the bobbing forms of several riders, trying to urge more speed from their used-up mounts.

Without stopping, Harlan studied the coming horses, saw they were doing more lunging in the deep sand beneath the snow than they were actual running; steam from their overheated bodies joined their frosty breaths and encircled them and their riders in a menacing, rolling fog. "Git going, gal," he yelled as he lit into the dun's rump with the rope again. "We're going to make a run for it, slick or not! When we top out I'll unload the dun an' ride him. With two fresh horses we should be able to gain some ground on 'em. Their horses are as wrung out as mine is, maybe more so."

And it might have worked, except for one thing: J.W. Cain knew the country too well. When he saw that old man was turning into Minneosa Canyon he told two men to stay on top, ride like hell, and block off the trail that led out of the canyon to the east. That was the trail that Harlan and Tracey were clambering up, scattering rocks and snow and bits of broken hoofs. They were but ten feet from the summit when Cain's riders came to a haunch-burning, rock-throwing stop above them.

"Pull up, Tracey," Harlan said with resignation,

"looks like all the cards has been dealt this hand. Now it's time to see who's got what."

The riders on the canyon floor were now only a quarter mile from the foot of the trail; the ones on the rim sat quietly with guns drawn. "Tracey, ain't no need lying to you, we're in a hell of a jam. We never figured Cain'd put more'n one man on my trail." Harlan looked at the slim figure beside him, saw the fear in her eyes, saw her hands tremble. "No matter what happens here and now, you don't give up, you hear? Jesse sure as hell won't, and that I can promise you."

His eyes went back to the men below them. His horse was turned sideways in the trail, hiding his right hand from the men above. He eased his six-gun out of its holster, unfastened one button on his coat and slid the gun-clutching hand inside.

"No, Harlan," Tracey said when she saw him hide the gun, "please, not that! I'll tell Cain that I'll go with him without a fight, maybe . . ."

"Now you looky here, gal," Harlan said in a loud whisper, dead serious, "I ain't about to let you go with that devil just to keep me outa trouble. I done let you down once in Mobeetie, I ain't afixing to do 'er again. You just 'member what I said about not giving up, no matter what happens. And, Tracey, if you don't mind an' old man saying so . . . well, if I'd ever had a wife or a daughter, I'd a wanted 'em to be just like you."

Tracey, with tears on her cheeks said, "Harlan, I . . ."

"Never mind, Tracey," Harlan cut her off, "I know. You just remember that Jesse will be coming."

Cain and the riders with him were now coming up the trail. Harlan's hand tightened on the curved butt of the Colt, his thumb felt the serrations of its heavy hammer. If he could catch Cain at the right moment, he should be able to bring it out and get off a shot in one sweeping motion, before anyone had time to react. It wouldn't save his own life; he would go down in a storm of bullets from the other guns. But if he killed Cain, Tracey should be saved from whatever fate awaited her, before Jesse realized something had gone wrong and came back.

To protect and defend. Those were the reasons Harlan had now for living, and, as strange as it was even to him, they seemed just reasons for his dying. An unexpected calmness came over him—he would be dead soon, but that was not what his mind focused upon. Rather it was the desire to take J. W. Cain with him in death—not out of hate, for right now he felt none, but out of love.

J. W. Cain was now stopped twenty feet below, sitting in front of the other riders. "Well, now," he said, colder than any arctic wind that ever assailed the plains, "you old bastard, you're not smiling so much now that Garrett and East aren't here, are you?"

But Harlan did smile. He smiled as his thumb pressed down on the hammer and his arm moved in a sweeping, fluid motion. But even with the headstart Harlan had given himself, his weapon had not yet reached full-cock when Cain's hand dropped and came up, filled with exploding fury that sent horses into a frightened frenzy, sending rocks and snow cascading down the hillside as they twisted and reared at the booming report.

Cain's slug caught the old cowboy just under the right rib cage, plowed the width of his small frame and stopped just under the skin on the opposite side. The range was close, the bullet angling upward. Harlan was lifted enough from the impact that his horse spun out from under him in a sudden, downhill whirl. He landed face down, his lifeblood flowing freely into the snow, staining it a bright crimson and giving rise to small wisps of steam.

The old puncher's heart still beat though, and still harbored life and fight. As Tracey screamed his name and jumped from her horse, he was rising from the snow to hands and knees with blood gushing from his nose. His six-gun was a foot downhill from his hand, and though he still had the will to save the girl clawing her way to him in panic, falling, rising, crying, and falling again, his will could no longer control his muscles. His old hand moved toward the gun, but slowly.

J. W. Cain watched the tortured movements of the old man and the panic-stricken rush of the girl, but his stone-cold heart felt no compassion.

When Harlan's hand at last touched the steel of his revolver, J. W. Cain's Colt was raised and cocked a second time.

The second time the canyon reverberated with gunshot, it was mercifully beyond even the damnable prowess of J. W. Cain to prolong Harlan's agony another heartbeat. The small form that had held so much joy and spirit now lay empty, never again to quicken another soul with laughter.

CHAPTER 21

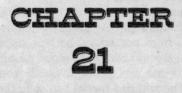

Harlan had been gone from the herd for an hour, an hour of silence except for the rattle of hoofs, the yells of the men to keep the cattle moving, the occasional cussing directed at a wandering-off cow. Jim East, riding drag with Jesse, had looked at him a few times and grinned; Jesse had returned the grins, but neither man had said anything. After another half hour of this East broke the silence with: "Jesse, I won't even ask how the hell you got those fresh-branded cows in the canyon without Cain knowing about it, but I am going to ask you how you intend to get the cows away from the county."

"Well," Jesse began, "I don't have a plan for that. I guess I knew J. W. Cain was a thief and couldn't be counted on to do the right thing. Now I guess I'll find out about Oldham County."

They drove the cattle in silence for a few more minutes, then East loped around the herd to where Pat Garrett was riding point, talked to him for another half hour, then motioned for Jesse to join them.

"Coldiron," Garrett said when Jesse reined in beside them, "Jim here still allows as how you're a damned good feller and that maybe we owe you a favor. I can't say that I see either one of them things as a fact, but, as a favor to Jim," here the tall Ranger emphasized *Jim* so that Jesse wouldn't get the wrong idea, "here's what I'll do: With any luck we should be in Tascosa by dark. At ten o'clock in the morning, you be at the courthouse; I'll try to have the county judge and the commissioners there, too. I'll lay it out for 'em, the way it really is. You can have your say, too. Then, it'll be up to them. Whatever they decide is the way it'll be, and I sure as hell don't make any promises about which way they'll go."

So that was the way it was going to be, thought Jesse. Okay. After all he had been through to get the cattle to this point, it would all come down to a decision by the Boss Ranchers—for Jesse believed that the decision made by the county commissioners would only mirror the decision made by the big cattlemen. But for some reason he had a good feeling about the next morning's meeting.

As he rode back to the drag of the herd he looked toward the west. Tracey and Harlan should be catching up with them soon, and he was anxious to share the semi-good news with them. He had no way of knowing, of course, that Harlan's catching-up days were all finished, and that Tracey, instead of coming to meet him, was riding in the opposite direction knowing that the gates of Hell had just slammed shut behind her.

By mid-afternoon, when they still had not shown

up, Jesse was more than a little uneasy. By late afternoon, when they were still seven or eight miles from Tascosa, he knew that he had to go back and look for them. He loped to the front of the herd and told Jim East and Pat Garrett that fact.

"Coldiron," Garrett said, irritated and not trying to hide it, "I'm not telling you your business, but I'll tell you this: if any of those commissioners see you helping us drive these cattle into town, things might go a little better for you at that meeting tomorrow. You better think about it."

"I'm doing what I gotta do," Jesse replied. "I can't help what the commissioners might or might not see, I've gotta go back."

As he loped off Garrett yelled, "If you're not there at ten in the morning, Coldiron, I'll guarantee you you'll never get these heifers back."

Seven days had passed since Jesse's release from jail. Most of those seven days had been spent in the saddle, and but one horse had carried that saddle those seven days. The wear and tear and the miles were telling on that horse. It seemed to Jesse that with each saddling the flank cinch had to go a hole higher before it made contact with Jug's belly. This day had been no easier for the honest brown. Though the riding had not been hard, it had been steady ever since the saddle blanket fell on his back before daylight. Even with all of those considerations, Jesse knew that now was no time for slow riding. He put the horse in a long trot and let him gather the miles. As hilltop, draw, creek, and hilltop fell behind with no sign of riders coming toward them he grew more and more apprehensive.

A few clouds had formed just after dark but had since vanished, and now a full moon drifted in a clear, cold sky above a clear, cold world. In spite of the fact that the sun had shown all day long, the temperature had not risen enough to keep skim-ice out of a water bucket at midday, much less melt the snow cover on the ground. The full moon throwing its blue light over that snow gave the night more than enough illumination for Jesse to plainly see the dugout from the rim of Minneosa Canyon. But no sign of life could he detect there, no smoke curled out of its stovepipe, no candlelight shown out of its small window. The sure knowledge that the dugout was dark and cold caused his heart to leap to his throat. And it was still there when Jug took a few steps down the trail and then suddenly, with catlike quickness, snorted, whirled, and bolted back uphill, spooked by the sight and smell of death.

Jesse had lived only a partially civilized existence most of his life. He had seen many faces of death and thought he was hardened toward all of them. But when he rolled the stiffened body of Harlan Harrell over and saw the bloody contorted death mask on the once-merry face he became sick. He stepped away and leaned over while his stomach wrenched and convulsed itself empty.

Where Jesse had not panicked when it had been his own life hanging in the balance in the face of death, he now did. Then, there had been no time to dwell on what was happening. Out of an instinct for survival he had been forced into immediate actions that had kept his mind tuned only to the pressing seconds at hand and to what his reflexes were doing. Now, with Harlan's life already forfeited and Tracey's life—even her very soul—on the edge of an abyss maybe worse than death, there was nothing to divert his mind from a helpless, hopeless panic. His burden was all the greater because he knew that until he had arrived on the scene Harlan had been content to live out his healthy old age trapping predators, and Tracey, although far from content, had been able to keep the predator that stalked her from rushing and pouncing. Now, he felt he alone was responsible for forcing J.W. Cain to vent his murderous rage on an old man and—here Jesse's stomach knotted again from the mere thought—his maniacal lust and savage vengeance on Tracey.

Jesse draped Harlan's body over his saddle and led the snorting Jug down the trail. His cattle, his dream of independence, his prideful talk about not leaving until he had reclaimed what was wrongfully taken from him now seemed empty and selfish.

By the time he reached the dugout, however, a change had come over him. He could now see the obvious fact that the tracks left by the horses, with Tracey's paint no doubt in their midst, could be easily followed in the snow. Depending on the destination of those tracks, he *could* have the rest of the night to catch up with them. As long as Cain was traveling, Jesse felt that Tracey would be safe.

This gave Jesse a glimmer of hope and drove back his despair. The hope was a slim one, to be sure. But it was a slim hope in a stout heart, and it created a hundred and seventy pounds of hard-twisted resolve. Only the cold bottom of its own grave would keep that resolve from freeing Tracey and bringing J. W. Cain's overdrawn ledger sheet to balance.

Before Jesse could leave Minneosa Canyon though, there was something that had to be tended to. He knew he was being followed when he first left East and Garrett. He never saw the man, but he knew.

He knew it every time he topped a tall hill or ridge and Jug insisted on twisting around to look behind them with his ears perked up. There was no doubt that he had seen something back there, and it didn't take much to figure out what. In fact, Jesse would have been surprised if he had not been followed.

But now the matter had to be settled.

He laid Harlan's body beside the horse corral, ran inside the dugout and lit a candle on the table, then ran back outside and waited, with rifle in hand, behind a seven-foot-square hunk of former rimrock that was now sixty feet from the front of the dugout.

He did not have to wait long.

The man, whoever he was, had done his job about as well as anyone could have, Jesse had to give him credit for that. He had stayed out of sight, at least out of human sight, but stayed close enough to not lose his man.

When the man saw that Jesse's tracks went down into the canyon he stopped at the top of the trail and studied. Then the man backed off from the rim and in a few minutes reappeared on it again, this time above the dugout. From there he could see the faint yellow light coming out of the window and the single horse in the corral. Now, convinced that it was safe to go down the trail he had shied from minutes earlier, he loped back to it and came off. When he reached the spot on the hillside where there were many tracks and much blood he stopped, studied awhile, and then came cautiously on.

Jesse watched as the man dismounted a few hundred yards up the creek and hobbled his horse against a tall cutbank where it could not be seen from anyone around the dugout. The next time Jesse saw him he was coming up out of the creek, bent over, half-running, dodging prickly pear and bear grass.

The man was tall and very thin, and, just as sure as the night had become deathly quiet, Jesse knew who it was. Slim hurried toward the dugout, stopped, and hunkered down when he was a hundred and fifty feet behind it. He stayed there for five minutes, waiting, listening. Then he skirted around to his left until he was a hundred feet away, but now with a front view of the dugout, the horse corral, the dead man, and the square hunk of old rimrock.

Slim hunkered behind a big sagebrush and was motionless as a burned-out stump for another five minutes. Then he gathered himself, reached up and pulled the front of his hat down, and raced, still bent over, to the corner of the corral, only ten feet from Harlan's body and thirty feet from both the lighted window in front of him and the big square rock behind him.

Slim pulled his gun out of its holster, circled the corral, talked in soothing whispers to the brown horse, and then darted—stooped over extra low—to the front of the dugout where he knelt below the window. He stayed that way for a minute, then scraped off his hat and lifted one eye just above the bottom of the window frame.

While Slim peered in the window, Jesse stepped out to stand beside the square rock, on the moonlit side, raised his Winchester and eased back the hammer. As bright as the moon over the snow was, it was still not like aiming in daylight. But at sixty feet it was possible to center the figure in front of the dugout in the notch of the rear sight and rest the front blade where his chest would be when he whirled around.

"Slim," Jesse said just loud enough to be heard, like he was talking across a card table, but plenty loud to make Slim bunch his muscles and freeze, "I'd just as soon leave you here tied up and alive. If you want that, all you gotta do is drop that gun in the snow and tell me where Cain's headed. If you don't want that, Slim, I can leave you here without having to tie you up. Now you decide quick because I ain't got much time."

Until then, Slim had done everything about right. But when he heard Jesse's proposition and the cold voice on which it was announced, it was not using the best judgment to turn around without first planting his revolver in the snow. But it was still not the worst possible judgment because he turned around slow and with the gun uncocked.

The two men stood facing each other under the cold moon and in the stillness of the canyon; Jesse, with his Winchester hard against his shooting shoulder, the Dupont powder only eight ounces of trigger-pressure from igniting, and Slim, with his uncocked Colt at waist-level weighing his options.

Then Slim used the worst possible judgment. He raised the Colt and thumbed back the hammer. Jesse gathered those other eight ounces of trigger pressure in less than a heartbeat and his Winchester exploded a split second before Slim's Colt.

Slim's bullet went into the air and Jesse's went between two ribs on the right side. Slim was spun around but kept his feet under him and his long fingers around his Colt. When he came around again he sent a bullet only inches from Jesse's face. Jesse levered home a fresh cartridge without taking the rifle from his shoulder and the Winchester spoke again.

CHAPTER

22

Jesse had some traveling to do and he set his mind to that task and nothing else. Judging from the condition of the tracks and Harlan's frozen blood, he knew Cain had a several-hour head start on him. This being the case, and Jesse being a man who scratched out his living by knowing what horses were capable of, he knew better than to rush off at a run. Instead, it was in a trot, again, that he put the big gelding; a long-strided trot that covers the miles at a steady rate but does not quickly drain the energy.

With a firm set to his jaw and a steady eye on the tracks, Jesse realized that the hand he now held was the one that he must play through to the end, win or lose. If he had to discard a horse now he could not draw another. On top of that, all the cards were faceup—there would be no bluffing now. The stakes were the highest possible: life or death.

So the unassuming, slender cowboy and the big brown gelding beneath him settled into a trot, mile after mile falling behind them. Jesse shifted his weight from the saddle seat to the stirrups, from the back and kidneys of Jug to his powerful shoulders.

On and on they followed the tracks as the sign left the riverbed and angled southwest. When he could, Jesse let Jug drink from a spring or a stream. The miles receded behind them at five an hour, hour after hour.

Across barren, open flats; rocky canyons; lonely ridges; mesquite thickets; cedar brakes; always south by west.

Across wide and sandy Trujillo Creek in the moonlight.

Across the wandering and twisting Canadian River again, and then by dark-shadowed, silent and decaying Salinas Plaza, home only of packrats and things that feed on packrats.

Leaving the skeletal remains of Salinas behind, Jesse followed the tracks across the Canadian River yet another time and into Tucalo Canyon.

Then out of Tucalo Canyon and back to the north side of the river. But now it was not just a small band of horses he was following. Now it was the herd of cattle, also. And now the tracks turned westward and went through deep sand, tall sagebrush, and less and less snow.

The meaning of the herd of cattle was quickly grasped by the lone rider following its cold wake, and it was welcome news: Driving a herd of cattle is much slower going than merely riding across the range in a long trot. Now, Jesse figured, he could gain ground on J. W. Cain.

But bad news was hard on the heels of the good. The invisible line separating Texas and the Territory of New Mexico had to be crossed with a gentle coaxing of steel. Spurs now had to be used on Jug where they never had to be used before. For eighteen hours the tall gelding had been under the saddle; over seventy miles of rock and sand. And if spurs were now needed it was not because of lack of heart—it was because of disobedient, oxygen-starved muscles and aching, stiff joints.

Panhandle snow had become New Mexico sand, but it was sand that held hoof prints almost as readily as snow, and revealed them almost as readily in the blue moonlight. That blue moonlight, however, did not promise to last the whole night through. The moon was sinking fast and Jesse knew, with a returning knot in the pit of his stomach, that a spent horse pulling through deep sand would be no match for a setting moon on a downhill plunge.

Just as the moon set, Cain and the herd arrived at his ranch in New Mexico Territory. A better sanctuary for a man in the type of cattle enterprise that J.W. Cain was involved in there never was—it was out of reach of Texas law and a hundred miles east of any seat of government in the Territory.

Throughout all the cold hours of night travel the loop of Cain's rope had remained snug around the neck of Tracey's paint horse. A few times he had turned in his saddle to look at her, but never did he speak. As for Tracey, she had made no sound—not one syllable said, not one sob released—since the piercing scream when Harlan had died in front of her.

Though somewhat in a state of shock, Tracey's mind was not so numbed to the point where she did not realize what was happening, or what had happened, or what would happen when they reached their destination. As for the future, her mind was short-circuited with conflicting thoughts. Of course she wanted this nightmare to pass soon and for her and Jesse to live happily ever after. But logic told her that this could never be, that the clock marking their time together had already ticked away their allotted time. Their next step had two possibilities, both equally dark: Either Jesse would never find her, or if he did he would be killed. She hoped he would never find her, for she could not bear the thought of Jesse dying.

She had no sooner convinced herself of this, though, when she realized something else. It was only a feeling coming from deep within her, but it was a feeling too strong to be denied—whether she wanted him to or not, Jesse would come to her, she would love him all the more for it . . . and then she would see him die.

Once they arrived at the ranch, Cain released the cattle at a water hole, posted guards around his headquarters, and took Tracey straight to his big frame house. With a hand gripped tightly around a slender arm he led her down a dark hall and into an equally dark room.

Tracey could see nothing in the darkness. Her arm was released. She heard the door shut and a key rattle in its lock. Her heart screamed for her to run, but there was nowhere to run to. She could not see a sliver of light. She had no way of knowing which side of the door Cain was on when it was locked. Maybe he was not in the room—or maybe he was standing beside her, reaching to touch her.

For ten long minutes the young woman stood in the darkness and the silence without moving, terrorized by the unknown. Then utter exhaustion and strain wilted her to a hard floor where she lay sobbing and cold.

Time had no meaning for Tracey and she did not

know whether she had been huddled on that lonely floor for a few minutes or a few hours when she heard the rattle of a key in the lock again.

The door opened and J. W. Cain's form was silhouetted against the light in the hall. The door closed, darkness returned, and she heard him walking across the room.

A match was struck. It flared to life and the big hand holding it held it to a lantern. Tracey stood and then backed against a boarded-over window.

Cain nonchalantly fired a cigar and grinned. "Tracey, you don't need to be afraid of me; I only want to be good to you." After a pause he said, "Look the room over."

Tracey's eyes had already been taking in the room by the dim light of the single lantern: the brown curtains covering the boarded-over window, the wagon-wheel chandelier, the oak chest of drawers with brass pulls, the elegantly carved oak headboard of the bed, the blue-and-white checkered quilt, the gray walls. Somehow all of these things stirred an old memory she could not place.

"Do you recognize anything, Tracey?" Cain asked politely. "I'll be disappointed if you don't."

When Tracey did not speak, he went to the chest of drawers, took something out of the top drawer, and tossed it on the bed. "Maybe this will help your memory."

Tracey looked at the thing and tightened. It was a red satin dress bordered in black. A saloon-girl's dress, tiny at the waist and low-cut in front.

"Why?" she gasped.

"You do recognize it then. That's good, Tracey. I went to a lot of trouble to make everything the same as it was that night. That's even the very same dress;

if you remember, you left in too much of a hurry to take it with you. I had the rips in it fixed and I'm dying to see if it looks as good on you now as it did five years ago."

"But why?"

"Why? I thought if we could start over with everything just like it was that night our relationship would be a lot smoother. Well, I mean to make a few changes here and there, of course. Oh, you'll notice that not *everything* is the same—I left out the razor. But, don't be frightened, Tracey. Like I said, I don't mean to hurt you. Let's just start over, Tracey, and you'll see how good I can make things for you."

Tracey's defiance rose. "Do you think I'd *ever* willingly be your woman?"

"Yes," Cain said confidently, softly, "I think, in time, you will be very willing to be my woman—after a period of adjustment, of course. Tracey, I'll give you things you never dreamed of and take you to places you don't even know exist."

"Aren't you forgetting something?" asked Tracey.

Cain's smile quickly left his face. His fingers involuntarily touched the long red scar on his cheek. "I never forget *anything*, Tracey."

"What about Jesse?"

"I promised to send him to hell and I will."

"If I promise to be your woman willingly like you said, will you not kill him?"

"That depends on how much of a woman you are and how willing."

Tracey forced a smile. "I can be a lot of woman, J.W.—more than you know."

J. W. Cain smiled. "Are you ready to show me now?"

"Does Jesse live?"

"As long as you make me happy—only that long."

"And if he comes here to get me?"

Remembering his last instructions to Slim, Cain said, "I wouldn't worry about him showing up here if I were you. But if he does, you tell him how it is between me and you. If you convince him and he leaves, then he lives. If I even *think* you might not make me happy, he dies like that old man did. Now, it would make me real happy for you to put on this red dress. Right now."

"But . . . but I need a little time, J. W. Just a little while to . . ."

"Just in case Coldiron shows up this morning I'll have to be convinced that you mean what you say, Tracey. . . . Now come over here and I'll help you get out of those ugly clothes."

Tracey needed no time to convince herself that the trade she had negotiated was the only course of action for her, but she required a long minute to gather enough nerve and move across the room to where J.W. Cain stood.

She walked slowly and came to stand silently next to him. He smiled and leaned over and kissed her neck while she died inside. Then a pair of big hands moved to the top button on her shirt and fumbled with it. Tracey stood still and bit her lip while the other four buttons were loosened and the shirt was pulled over her shoulders.

Cain's eyes widened at the sight of her tender flesh. His voice became dry and raspy. "I'll think we'll save the dress for tonight."

When she was led to the bed Tracey's stomach was in her throat and she barely held back a scream.

When a hand touched the top button on her britches a muffled sob escaped her trembling lips.

The top britches button popped open. The sweaty hand that opened it came to rest on the second. Tracey's sob burst into a scream that she could not hold back. "No!" she cried, "No! No!" She covered her tan face with slender hands and kicked at everything and nothing, uncontrollably, with her feet.

A wildly kicking foot landing squarely in the groin has the same effect as an aimed one. A grimace clutched Cain's face as he doubled over. His face grew pale, while the cheek scar darkened and twitched.

When an enraged J. W. Cain straightened and came toward her, Tracey sat up and tried to dodge, but she was no match for a man who was twice her own weight. A driving hard-knuckled fist caught her right eye. She snapped backward so hard she completely flipped off the bed, landing facedown on the hard floor, unmoving.

"Mr. Cain." It was a voice from in front of the house. "I think you better come out here."

Cain, wild-eyed and breathing in excited short gasps, sprang to stand astraddle the limp form of Tracey Coldiron. He took off his wide belt and eyed her small, tan back.

"Mr. Cain!" This time the voice was louder and more urgent. "I'm telling you you'd better come look at this!"

CHAPTER

23

When he stepped off the porch and joined the two guards in front of the house, J. W. Cain's composure had returned. "Coy," he said, "this better be important. I put you in charge until Slim gets back and I expect you to handle things without my help. Now, what in the hell is it that's so important?"

Coy, a cowboy of about thirty with refined, clean features and a long nose, pushed his hat back and gestured with his head toward the south. "I figured you'd be wanting to take a look out yonder for yourself," he said.

"Where?" said Cain with an irritated tone that faded into the cold morning breeze as his eyes followed Coy's to the south, past the front gate and out into the sage beyond.

There, two hundred yards in front of the big gate, in the dim twilight, was a man on a horse. A lone man sitting motionless atop a big horse that held its head low. A lone man who watched the Cain headquarters with the simple curiosity of a wild animal.

"How long's he been out there?" asked Cain with interest.

By this time the man who had been on duty at the gate had joined them and it was he who answered: "Not but a little bit, I don't think. I don't know where he come from. One minute there wasn't nothing out there plumb to the end of the draw, then I rolled a smoke an' when I look back out yonder, there he was. He's jist been sitting there like he is now ever since I first seen him. At first I thought it was Slim, but it ain't."

"No," Coy agreed, studying the figure, "it ain't Slim. Not near tall 'nough. I can't figure who the hell it is though, or how come he's just a sittin' there. Damn funny thing if you ask me."

A rustle and a sliding sound behind the men caused them to turn toward the porch. They saw Tracey leaning against a post. She had a blanket wrapped around herself and her gaze, at least from the eye that was not swollen shut and bleeding, was on the man sitting quietly in the sagebrush.

"Jesse," she whispered.

"Good God!" exclaimed Coy. "What happened to her, Mr. Cain?"

"Jesse," Tracey whispered again.

"It's none of your business," Cain said to Coy, "what happened to her. I tell you what your business is and what it's not. And this is not."

All eyes then shifted back to the lone man in the wide draw.

"He's getting out his rifle, looks like to me."

Coy turned to Cain and said, "That man out yonder's Coldiron, ain't it, Mr. Cain?"

Once the man had the rifle out and laid across his saddle he grew as still as before. The wind moved the sagebrush in the draw. It tugged the mane and tail of the brown horse and plucked the loose ends of the man's neckerchief and coattail, but that was all that moved anywhere up and down that long, wide draw.

"He 'minds me of a Co-manch warrior," said a man in front of the house, "jist sitting out there an' staring."

Tracey could scarcely see her husband through the one good eye but she knew it was him. To her, he looked as sad and lonesome as he had sounded that night beside the river in Tascosa. How she longed to hold him just once more. Just once more to feel his arms around her and to feel safe and loved. But she knew that could never be. She reached out a small hand as though she might touch him across the two hundred yards that separated them. She reached out the trembling hand and whispered, barely moving her lips, "Jesse . . . turn around and leave now, please. Don't come closer. Please, Jesse, don't die."

Four men came out of the bunkhouse and joined the others in front of the house. They rubbed blood-shot eyes and looked at the battered woman on the porch, and then they looked toward the man in the draw. To all of them—except for J. W. Cain—the man out there looked like a man about to die, but a brave man nonetheless.

To J. W. Cain, the man in the draw looked like a man about to die all right, but a damn fool of a man.

"Yeah," Cain said after a while, "that's Coldiron." Then Cain pulled out his Colt, checked the cartridges in it by slowly turning the big cylinder, and then dropped it back into its holster.

"Coldiron," yelled Cain, "come on up here so I can see your face when you die."

The metallic sounds of a Winchester lever being

pulled down and then driving a cartridge into the chamber came on the cold morning air to the men in front of the house. It came crisp and clear from the draw.

"Goddamn," one of the men in front of the house said.

"He's coming this way now," said another, "just walking that horse like he was in downtown Dodge."

"Jesse! No!" cried out Tracey. She stepped off the porch and started to run toward him but instead fell at the feet of the cluster of men.

"Get her, Coy!" demanded Cain. "Keep her out of the way, but keep her out here. I want her to see this."

Coy helped Tracey to her feet and led her to the side.

"I want the first shot," Cain said, "but after I open up the ball, all of you boys can join in."

Coy looked at Tracey's bloody, swollen face. Then he looked at the rest of the men, and finally he looked at his boss and said, " 'While ago you said this was none of my business, an' I reckon you're right. None of this is any of my business. This is between you an' that man out in the draw, and I don't reckon I'll chip in at all. But I will keep this woman outa the way."

Cain looked hard at Coy, and then he looked hard at the other men. All of them, all the way down to Big Perce, nodded and looked at the ground in silent agreement with Coy. For the most part, this cluster of men were cowboys who had slipped over the thin line that separated the law-abiding from the law-breaking in the aftermath of the failed cowboy strike, but they were not woman beaters. And they respected bravery above most other virtues. If the man sitting out there in the frosty sage wanted to ride in and get himself killed that was his business, but he deserved a chance to die in a fair fight.

"Well, I'll be. . . ." growled Cain. "Coy, I'll deal with you later. I sure as hell won't need any help with one dim-witted cowboy—I just thought you boys might need a little excitement. Now I'm thinking that you might be needing something else, like a new job and a new man to sponge off of."

Jesse was now walking Jug through the big front gate. Cain stepped forward a few feet, and the men around him stepped back and to the side.

"Where's Slim, Coldiron?" Cain yelled. "Did you backshoot him?"

Jug walked forward, his tired head hanging low and the cowboy on his back as silent as the prairie around them.

When seventy-five feet separated them Cain yelled, "This is some woman you got for a two-dollar marriage license, Coldiron. I guess that's about all she's worth, though. She's spoiled something awful. It'll take me a long time to get her straightened out and teach her some discipline. But what the hell, I've got plenty of time to work on it. Too bad you can't stick around and see how it's done."

Fifty feet separated them now. The first rays of the morning sun touched the tops of the cottonwoods around the house and the tops of the hills on either side of the draw. The breeze that had been stirring had stopped and now not even the soft tips of the sagebrush moved.

"Coldiron, I think you ought to look behind you. You must have left your lawmen friends in Texas, and now there's not a goddamn soul to save your neck."

Jesse came on, unhurried, his countenance unchanged as the big land surrounding them.

At forty feet, Jesse took his eyes off J. W. Cain and looked at Tracey. Only then did he see the blood and the awful bruises on her face.

At thirty feet, Jesse dug his spurs into Jug's belly with terrible force. The big brown lurched forward and, in spite of his weariness, did so with incredible swiftness. In two steps he was at full speed.

When Jug shot forward, Cain's hand dropped to the gun on his hip. Jesse and Jug were still fifteen feet away when the Colt cleared leather and came up cocked.

Jesse raised his rifle, but he was two seconds behind Cain's Colt. It was plain to see what the next second would bring. It would bring death to Jesse Coldiron in an ear-splitting report.

But not so. Not so because when Cain's hand dropped, Tracey jumped forward. Only by utter command of will over muscle did her small body, beaten and weakened, find the strength to jerk from the grasp of Coy and bolt to the muzzle of J. W. Cain's Colt. The instant his finger tightened on the trigger is when her hands grabbed his weapon and forced it down.

The shot, the ear-splitting report that would have never been heard by Jesse but for Tracey's sacrifice, was now muffled by her body. The blanket around her was scorched by the burning gunpowder. The bullet threw her backwards and knocked her to the ground, unmoving.

When Tracey was hurled backwards by Cain's bullet, Jug was no more than five feet away and racing toward the smoking gun. Cain thumbed back the hammer and pulled the trigger again. It was a shot taken in desperation at the onrushing mass of muscle and brown hair, but it was a shot not likely missed.

The heavy bullet shattered Jug's massive left shoulder, and he could not have fallen any faster if both legs had been shot off at the knees. So quickly did he go down that the man in front of him had no chance to jump aside, and Jesse had even less chance to step out of the saddle. All three went down in a mass of dust, brown hair, flying hoofs, and blood.

The next heartbeat found dust hanging in the air, Jug kicking wildly on his side, Jesse's leg pinned underneath Jug, and Cain on his back in the dirt.

In a frantic race two men scrambled for instruments of death. A big, sure hand streaked for a Colt revolver two feet away. A sunburned and callused hand reached half that distance for a Winchester rifle.

Cain's hand consumed but the tiniest fragment of time in starting the Colt up and its deadly hammer back.

But the sunburned hand had the lesser distance to move, and while the hammer of the Colt was still turning its cylinder the Winchester hammer was already on its short journey home.

Suddenly the man behind the Colt knew the panic he thought was for lesser men. In a fleeting second between life and death he felt rather than saw the meeting of the other hammer and its waiting firing pin.

With eyes wide and disbelieving Cain felt his chest take the full energy of a .44 caliber rifle at ten feet, felt the burning as 200 grains of powder-heated lead drove deep into his very own blood and bone. He was knocked back two steps, breathing blood, but his hand still gripped the Colt and again he tried to bring it up.

The second muzzle blast from the Winchester was the last thing J. W. Cain saw and heard. His last vindictive curse was forever unfinished.

Jesse laid the rifle down and fell back with his leg still trapped beneath the still and quiet Jug. He looked up at the clear blue sky and he smelled the frost on the sage, but no joy did he feel in being alive to do either. And no victory did he feel in having killed J.W. Cain. He had come to save Tracey or to die, and he had failed to do either. Like nothing he had ever felt before, he felt the emptiness of that failure. It was an inside emptiness as great as if he had been lying dead upon the open prairie until he was nothing but brittle rawhide stretched over a collapsing skeleton. He had no will now to live, and the thought of his own carcass drying in the sun was somehow the only thought that held no pain. His hand felt the hard side of the Winchester and closed around it.

"Jesse?" It was a small, weak voice behind him.

He turned his head and there was a bloody face looking at him and a trembling hand reaching out to him.

"Tracey!" Jesse said, gladness filling the vacuum in his heart. "You're alive!"

"Yes," she said softly, "alive. And so are you." She grimaced in pain. "We're alive, Jesse. We're alive."

CHAPTER
24

J. W. Cain's death rattle had scarcely quieted before his men were saddling their horses and riding away either alone or in small groups. Like Jesse, they knew their business was finished at the Cain Ranch. Jesse neither knew nor cared where they were going.

He cared only that Tracey was alive. And by a matter of only a few inches she would live. Had Cain's gun discharged an instant before it did, she would have received a fatal wound in the abdomen. As it was, she had forced his hand down enough so that the bullet struck her just below the groin, where it went through two inches of soft flesh on the inside of the left thigh.

Quickly—for he feared that some of Cain's thieves might reconsider and think it foolish to let them leave— Jesse packed her wound with his neckerchief to stem the bleeding. Then he went to the horse corral and caught three horses: Harlan's sorrel, Tracey's paint, and his little packhorse.

In ten minutes he had them saddled and was riding

toward the east, leading the paint and the packhorse and carrying Tracey in his arms.

He stopped often to see to Tracey's wound and to let his aching arms rest, but he never made camp until they reached the dugout in Minneosa Canyon at midnight.

So exhausted and weak was Tracey when Jesse laid her on the bunk that she slept most of thirty-six hours straight. Jesse was nearly as exhausted but slept only in short stretches and was at her side every time she moaned. He kept the bullet hole opened up so it would drain and heal from the inside. Even so, for three days Jesse could see no change in her weakened state, and he began to fear that infection had too firm a hold on her.

Then almost overnight she began to improve. Her appetite returned; she grew stronger; her smile became brighter and brighter. It was then that she tried to persuade Jesse to go to Tascosa and reclaim the cattle.

Jesse would only grin. He would not consider leaving her alone and still far from healed.

If he seemed quite unconcerned about the cattle it was because he knew there was nothing to be concerned about. He knew that shortly after he had missed the meeting Garrett was to have set up with the county commissioners, the Boss Ranchers would have seen to it that the cattle were gone. It was not in their nature to show compassion for a tardy cowboy. He knew, even before he returned to the dugout with Tracey in his arms, that he would never see his heifers again.

But Jesse felt no sense of loss. How could he? In the slender, long-haired woman slowly regaining her strength he had found what he had been searching for all of his life. All those years he had believed the treasure of the sage to be a herd of his own cattle grazing upon it. He had been wrong—it was a good woman with whom to love and to share that quietness. A woman who loved him so much she was willing to lay down her life for him. A woman who asked for nothing, yet was willing to give everything. Tracey had cured the restless longing in him that a hundred head of heifers had not. There would be other heifers; they were born by the thousands every spring. But Tracey was the one woman who could give meaning to his life and make it more than just a passing of time from the cradle to the grave in a harsh land.

The days passed swiftly by without them seeing another living soul. The terrible bruise on Tracey's eye turned blue, then green, then yellow. The bullet wound healed faster than Jesse had hoped and after ten more days Tracey was able to ride again.

"Now we'll go to Tascosa together," Jesse said, "just to keep 'em honest."

It was just past noon on a clear, cool day on the twenty-first of December when they trotted out of the cottonwoods along the creek just west of town. When they reached Main Street they were riding abreast and leading the dun packhorse. The wind at their backs was not strong by Panhandle standards but still it scooted and rolled volumes of dry leaves under and past them with a crisp rustling noise.

Jim East was walking in front of the businesses along Main Street when he looked up the street and saw them coming. He hailed them with a wave that brought them to the front of the Exchange Hotel, where he waited.

After a quick exchange of greetings, Jesse said, "I

thought you would want to know that Harlan's dead. He's buried in front of his dugout.''

East had been smiling but now turned serious. "Sorry, Jesse," he said. "What happened? Where've you been?"

Before Jesse could answer, three men stepped out of the hotel and joined them. The three were Pat Garrett, W. M. D. Lee, owner of the LS Ranch, and J. E. McAllister, Lee's general manager and an Oldham County Commissioner.

"Well, Coldiron," Garrett said, "I didn't think we'd be seeing you around here anymore. Not after all this time."

"I came to get my cattle," said Jesse bluntly.

"Have you now?" said a stern-faced W. M. D. Lee. "You should have been doing that a long time ago"—he looked at Tracey—"instead of gallivanting around."

Jesse put both hands over the saddle horn and relaxed. "I was tied up for awhile but I'm here now."

"Yeah," said J. E. McAllister, speaking with an air of authority, "we can see that, but it's a mite too late."

"Meaning what?" asked Jesse.

"Meaning," returned McAllister with a hard inspection of the mounted cowboy before him, "that if you had any legitimate claim to any cattle in possession of Oldham County you should have been here when we had a called meeting to discuss just that. Since you weren't we had to assume that you relinquished any claim you might of had. Meaning that laws are made to be kept and our laws allow us to sell or dispose of outlawed or unclaimed cattle as we see fit, and the cattle you're talking about would fit into either category.

"To not take up any more time than I have to, Coldiron, I'll shorten it for you as much as I can. The county sold the cattle in question and a couple hundred others and the money is on the way to a Kansas City bank to be placed in the county's account. And there's nothing anyone can do about it."

Jesse tightened, leaned forward in the saddle with his forearms across the horn, and stared at the ground while the men standing in front of him waited to see what his reaction would be to McAllister's harsh speech.

When Jesse looked up again he was smiling. "Now how in the thunder do you reckon I knew that's what you'd say?" he asked with a wink to Jim East.

"I'll give you a piece of advice, Coldiron," said W. M. D. Lee. "If a man is ever going to have anything in this life he has to learn to make some sacrifices."

The cowboy looked at the woman beside him and the faint bruise still on her face, then he looked back at W. M. D. Lee. "Is that so?" he said. "I'll sure try an' remember that, Mr. Lee."

When they started to rein their horses around Jim East said, "If you two need a place to put up, Jesse . . ."

"Thanks, Jim," said Jesse, "but it just so happens that I know where there's a pretty little Colorado canyon with nothing in it but a cabin that's chock-full of winter grub. I reckon we'll winter there. Come spring, we may go to Wyoming. Or we may try Arizona. Or maybe Dakota. Heck, we may just give the horses their heads and let 'em go where they want to. Harlan always said that a good horse had more sense than any cowboy when it came to finding a good place. We'll get the money from Harlan's critter scalps and I figure that Montana banker would rather me invest it than worry him with it."

"By the way," injected Garrett, speaking around a toothpick in his mouth, "where's that good brown horse you've been riding?"

"I guess you could say that I traded him off."

"Is that right?" said W. M. D. Lee, surprised. "I wish we'd a known that. We can always use good horses at the ranch."

Coldiron looked Mr. Lee in the eye and said, "You couldn't have afforded him."

"Say, Coldiron," snapped J. E. McAllister as if the thought just struck him, "we were just talking about J. W. Cain. It seems nobody's seen him lately—have you?"

Jesse wrinkled his eyebrows in thought. "No," he said, "not lately." Then he and Tracey turned and rode away.

EPILOGUE

It was never known for certain in Oldham County what became of J. W. Cain, the man who seemed bound for as much power and wealth as W. M. D. Lee. Most people believed that he became afraid of Pat Garrett and simply left the country while he could. But without first selling his house and little ranch west of town? That they couldn't answer. Others believed rumors about a band of outlaws catching him by surprise and murdering him and stealing his cattle. A few believed that the Panhandle Cattlemens' Association paid for his death. No one but Jim East even suspected that a common cowboy could have had anything to do with Cain's disappearance.

Nobody can say what became of Jesse and Tracey because when they rode out of Tascosa, they rode into oblivion. But a lot of people think their courtship was too brief and their marriage too hasty to survive for long. Wouldn't the reality of their situation—in debt, no job, no home—force them apart in a short while?

Some said this was so.

But they weren't there in the North Star Cafe on the fourth of December when Jesse and Tracey shared their first real smiles, when the slim cowboy hurled himself across a table of food to get to a giant of a man who had insulted the quiet girl. Nor were they down beside the river later, or in the home of Scotty Wilson, J. P.

And they weren't there on a brutal, frosty December seventh morning in New Mexico Territory to see what a man named J. W. Cain saw.

And they weren't there on the twenty-first of December, 1884—when Jesse and Tracey rode across a prairie many miles above the Canadian River as the sun was throwing long and cold shadows on the land, and dark clouds were looming in the north, and a faraway coyote's wail drifted over the hills as lost and lonesome-sounding as could be—to see how the couple rode so eagerly deeper and deeper into that giant land, and how they seemed so at home and so at peace in that vastness of sage and solitude and eye-hurting distance.

AUTHOR'S NOTE

The main characters in *The Long Season*—Jesse Coldiron, Tracey James, Harlan Harrell, J. W. Cain and his men—are fictitious. Jim East, Pat Garrett, Scotty Wilson, W. M. D. Lee and anybody mentioned as having a part in Oldham County politics were real persons, as was Mr. Sheets, owner of the North Star Cafe.

Not only in fiction were those violent times but in real life as well, as evidenced by the fact that both Pat Garrett and Jesse Sheets died suddenly and violently, the former after the turn of the century on a lonely New Mexico back road with two .45 slugs in him, and the latter on a night in March of 1886 when he stepped out of his North Star Cafe to see what a late-night ruckus was all about and died instantly when hit in the forehead by a bullet gone wild in an exchange of gunfire between LS cowboys and "Hogtown people." The incident left three other men dead.

Today Tascosa is but a memory—virtually the only building left is the rock courthouse built in 1884—but the country of the Canadian River breaks that stretches west of where Tascosa once was (home now to Cal Farley's Boys' Ranch) is not all that much changed from a hundred years ago. Every Spring up and down the Canadian the air is filled with the smoke from thousands of calves being branded, calves that are gathered by mounted cowboys and then roped and dragged to the branding fire as they always have been—and hopefully always will be.

SAM BROWN
Oldham County, Texas
1986

About the Author

Sam Brown has been a working cowboy most of his adult life. He started learning the ropes as a teen when he worked as a "dope boy." During cattle branding, he would carry a bucket of foul-smelling Black Widow Smear, with which he would dope or brush the calves (where they'd been dehorned or castrated) in order to prevent blow flies from laying eggs in the wounds. After a tour in the army, he taught school for a year, but the classroom was no match for the lure of the outdoors. In addition to cowboying full time for the Fulton *Quien Sabe* ranch, he is a veteran rodeo performer. He was one of three poets selected to represent his state at the Cowboy Poetry Gathering in Elko, Nevada, this year. *THE LONG SEASON* is his first published novel. Brown lives with his wife and two children in Adrian, Texas.